Jewish Latin America
Ilan Stavans, series editor

Cláper

Cláper

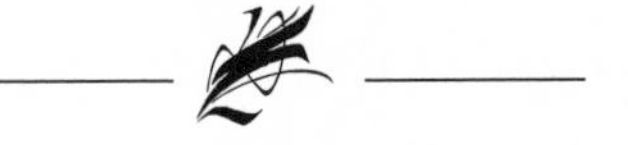

ALICIA FREILICH

Translated by
JOAN E. FRIEDMAN

Introduction by
ILAN STAVANS

University of New Mexico Press
Albuquerque

Library of Congress Cataloging-in-Publication Data

Freilich de Segal, Alicia.
[Cláper. English]
Cláper / Alicia Freilich ; translated by Joan E. Friedman.
p. cm.
ISBN 0-8263-1854-1 (cloth).—ISBN 0-8263-1855-X (pbk.)
1. Jews—Venezuela—Social life and customs—Fiction.
I. Friedman, Joan. II. Title.
PQ8550.29.E57C5513 1998
863—dc21

97-39916
CIP

Cláper is the second volume in the University of New Mexico Press series Jewish Latin America. The translator wishes to thank Naomi Lindstrom for her advice and friendship.

Introduction

ILAN STAVANS

Rereading Alicia Freilich's book set me thinking about the famous statement by Thomas Jefferson in the Declaration of Independence, the one about the unalienable, self-evident right that all men are entitled to the pursuit of happiness. It is the exact same reaction W. H. Auden had after reading *Red Ribbon on a White Horse,* the 1950 memoir of Anzia Yezierska. "I have read few accounts of such a pursuit so truthful and moving as hers," he claimed—and so do I, for *Cláper* is not only an immigrant story but a journey of self-discovery, a courageous attempt at building a home away from home and, in the process, being forced to reinvent everything we ever knew and felt.

Coupling Yezierska with Freilich might, at first sight, appear anachronistic, but it isn't; the two share not only the Polish landscape of their past but, also, a talent to describe in lyrical words the drama of immigrant departure and arrival. Yezierska, of course, experienced it first-hand. She is at least a generation older that Freilich. Born to a poor family in Plinsk, she moved to New York City's Lower East Side in the 1890s and it was there, amidst night classes and work in sweatshops, she began to write novels and short stories marked by an intensity of feeling, with characters—especially women—who yearn for dignity, respect, and independence. At the time of Yezierska's death, in 1970, Freilich was already thirty years old, teaching and dreaming of one day becoming a novelist. Caracas never had a Jewish ghetto, at least not of the type that comes to mind when one conjures Delancey and Hester streets. In fact, at the turn of the century the arrival of Jewish immigrants from Eastern Europe could hardly constitute a "wave"; it was more like an ocean spray—less than 2,000 by the end of World War II. But those who came struggled just the same with the duality of tongues and citizenship and, as *Cláper* testifies, with the shock of recognition. The manners of behavior they found were somewhat similar to the Russian and Polish spirits they had left behind: political volatility, an ingrained Catholicism, and a set of prejudices that included anti-Semitism. The static nature of Hispanic society seems to have depressed them at first; after all, much like in Europe, in the Southern Hemisphere an individual derives his sense of identity from his life-membership to a class. Of "Amerika," the English-speaking Paradise across the Atlantic, they had heard profusely; it was, in the words of cousins and friends that made it through Ellis Island, a country of hardship, restraining yet benign and penetrable, a place where status is temporary and success depends on achievement. Of *di anderer Amerique,* on the other hand, of the Spanish-speaking one they had just arrived into, they knew next to nothing—a Paradise Lost, tropical, exotic, a bit too colorful. Could they climb the social ladder just the same? Could achievement push them to the top without denouncing their ambition? And indeed, they soon realized that Latin America has always had problems with the concept of change. Mobility is arduous. Renewal comes in the form of violent breakthroughs. While the region, much as the United States, is the product of massive waves of newcomers, for complex historical reasons it doesn't fashion itself as an immigrant society. In it the immigrant is not a hero; neither is he a role model. All this, precisely, is why *Cláper,* in its English translation, is so valuable: first, because the immigrant novel per se is rare in the Southern Hemisphere; and second, because at its core, Freilich's is a profoundly Jeffersonian story written in a persistently undemocratic habitat, a contradiction that makes its pages all the more fascinating.

Born in Caracas in 1939, Freilich is the daughter of a Yiddish-speaking Pole much like Yezierska, a tongue-switcher who became a chronicler of Jewish life in South America and for decades served as correspondent for Abraham Cahan's *The Jewish Daily Forward.* A self-taught man of letters, he, Máximo Freilich—after whom Mordechai, a.k.a. Max, the protagonist of *Cláper,* is obviously modeled—was instrumental in building schools and community centers in Venezuela. More than anything, he turned the written word into his daughter's passion—or better, the written word*s*, since Yiddish was alive and well in the household, although Spanish was used in the public realm. Eventually she would grow up to become a schoolteacher, then the journalist she had hoped to turn into, and afterwards, a literary critic and novelist (*Cláper,* her first novel, came out in 1987).

The chronology of Jewish literature in Latin America is still being established, but a handful of truths are already evident. One is that writers were hardly read beyond their immediate circles, and each country had its own precursors appear at different times. For example, Alberto Gerchunoff was already a well-established Jewish figure in the Buenos Aires of the 1920s, way before any literary attempt in Spanish and Portuguese would occur in Mexico and Brazil. In this constellation, Venezuela, with its minuscule Jewish community, would take decades more. Another truth is that most first-generation Jewish writers in the region, all tongue-switchers, were well versed in the works of the Eastern European Yiddish masters (Mendele, Sholem

Aleichem, Peretz, et al.), as well as in the oeuvre of Russian geniuses like Tolstoy, Dostoyevsky, and Chekhov. But they had almost no connection with their own American counterparts (Cahan, Yezierska, and Henry Roth), mainly because English wasn't a tongue in their linguistic galaxy and translations were unavailable. *Call it Sleep,* for instance, did not appear in Spanish until 1990; and both *The Rise of David Levinsky* and *Bread Givers* remain unknown. Again, all this highlights Freilich's groundbreaking objectives in *Cláper:* to examine the labyrinthine paths of immigration in a civilization known for its xenophobia, to navigate the waters of transgenerational conflict while delving into the limits of secularism, and to connect the old and the new in an altogether unique Jewish-Venezuelan intercourse.

Transgenerational is a key word here. Polyphonic in style, *Cláper* is really made of two parallel monologues—Max's and his daughter's. The Venezuela that Max encounters after wandering around in Europe is filled with contradictions, a land of lost promises, astonished by its oil and natural riches but ungovernable. He finds it necessary to revisit his Polish *shtetl,* Lendov, in order to place tombstones on his parents' graves, but overwhelmed by the putrid smell of Hitler's Nazism, he returns to Caracas in 1938, thus closing his European past. He is able, in spite of all odds, to climb the economic ladder; and so, he is thankful. But his daughter will grow up to live the nation's contradictions more fully; in response, she will look back into the past and into memory for explanations. Through her own existential odyssey, she will bring the family puzzle together and, thus, add a new chapter to Venezuela's multiethnic history. Joan Friedman's English translation brilliantly conveys the intricacies of this double monologue, turning it into an enchanting dialogue. While Max's voice is oral Yiddish and his rhythm is that of a storyteller, his daughter's is analytical and overintellectualized Spanish, the speech a professional writer prudently selecting her words. In the clash of their languages and viewpoints, a new world is born.

The prodigal daughter, obviously, is Freilich herself, doing what Yezierska had done more than half a century before in a drastically different milieu: explain, with intensity of feeling, the ups and downs of an immigrant's pursuit of happiness—all in a language very much her own. In the end, the daughter's journey might have a deeper and more general significance today, for in a society where constant mobility is the rule and traditions are quickly eroding, children of displaced people, as Auden would say, have come to stand figuratively "as the symbol for Everyman."

Cláper

I'm happy. Through the clean mirror, as through pure crystal, I see that at last, yes, at last the sun is setting and the first evening star has come out. Shabbat ends but my night begins. All I want to do is walk and walk. . . .

I'm leaving you, my dear village, and you're seeing me off without knowing it. There is such excitement in your shabby narrow streets. This time Isaac and Pesha are the ones being led to the house of prayers. She will have to dance around him seven times before they shatter the glass in remembrance of the destruction of the temple in the Holy Land by the evilness of Titus the Roman. Cursed be his name! After hearing the noise and seeing the shards of glass, then and only then will they be man and wife according to the laws of our Arbiter, Creator of the Universe.

You know something? It's unusual for a month to go by without a wedding in my village. Nu? I guess even in Paradise it's not good to be alone. Why did I decide to leave at the end of this Shabbat and not another? I've waited long enough and the moment of destiny we forge for ourselves has arrived for me. . . .

But, I have to pretend and hurry without rushing. Thank god nobody notices as long as my mouth laughs and my legs dance by themselves, which is of course what happens to everyone in my village when there is a wedding. If I let myself be dragged into the merriment and forget my trip, I'll have to wait until next fall and that's too far away; after all I'm no longer a boy.

Is it true what they say, that a person's nature changes every seven years? If it is, then I've already shed my skin three times and I have reached the perfect age to break out of the shell forever. Forever? Do any of us ever really abandon forever the place where we're born and play as children?

A little while ago, on Yom Kippur, as I circled my head three times with the sacrificial rooster—and yelled out the exorcism louder than a crazy man would—I offered god this animal as a substitute for my sins. The bird will go to its death, that's what "capurot" is, after all, while I shall live a long and peaceful life in America. Amen!

Oy yoy yoy! Here comes Meilaj the mute. —Whew! He just passed. Thank you, my sweet little god, for your help. That good simpleton has very sharp eyes and with this full moon. . . . Luckily he didn't see me. He was so absorbed with his whistling, announcing the wedding and inviting all Christians to come and see the beautiful bride. Have you ever seen an ugly bride? Everyone praises such beautiful happiness! So, while performing his assignment with virtuosity, the whistler didn't notice me, leaving, with a knapsack over my shoulders.

As I pass the temple, I've got to walk more slowly. Awaiting the predestined couple, the wide open main door allows me to see the Ark which holds its treasure, the Holy Scrolls, on the very same dais where—oy yoy yoy!—so often, I've accompanied my Pappinyu at sunrise and sunset prayers.

God sits above and arranges it so that here, below, male and female may be joined at a chosen time. I know that all weddings are parties, but today the room looks more glittering than ever before. A couple of weeks ago from nobody knew where came a strange painter who decorated these blessed walls. And he never even charged us a cent! And, what's even more unbelievable, the drawings are intact!

I would look at him in silence because he was a man of few words. But one afternoon I took him some cider and sweet dough with raisins and, he spoke! He was fleeing France. He just wanted to breathe once again the air of Liozno, in Russia, where his family lives. But, when he realized how far away it was, he chose to remain in Lendov with us—"Almost the same"—he said, smiling, never once taking his eyes off the enormous rooster he was coloring blue.

Magical! That's what it was. Magical! Without any books, he knew exactly how to draw the feathers of all kinds of different creatures! From his brushes emanated a violin with wings, and green priests suspended in midair above roofs, and a seven-branched candelabra flying like a burning bramble, and a yellow lion and red cows, and gigantic moons, without a single word. Colored shapes with soul!

The entire town was shaken. So? Nu? Who was this stranger? Marcus Chagalovich or Sagalij he called himself, I no longer remember. Of course the village divided into two irreconcilable camps. One accused him of being a profligate and a sinner because of the irreverence with which he depicted the Sacred Commentaries. "Downright pagan!" The other said he had given a false name. They pointed him out as one of the anonymous Just Men who in every era come to redeem the world. Of course that would explain why he knew more about the Laws than our own venerable teacher Aaron.

Anyway, the artist was scared off by the whispers and all the gossips. After three days, probably to avoid being cursed by them—god forbid!—without even saying goodbye, or even leaving a single footprint, he disappeared into the night, just as I am doing now, along the very same long road. . . .

Luminous was the morning of her inauguration into the world! Without crossing checkpoints or oceans, and while living under the same familial roof, she took the road that divided Neighborhood from Milky Way.

She was not moved by her parent's objections nor, for that matter, did she share their mourning over the distant, yet to them, ever present news about the Suez Canal situation. Goodness, the way they moaned and carried on! You'd think these were their very own personal problems or something. . . .

The tree-lined path that leads to the main building with its high oval clock is both border and path to her liberation. There is a lot to see and many to be seen by. In order to accomplish this, she'll have to sway her hips and get rid of that skinny slouching profile, that "good-girl walk," Mom would say. A brave heroine, she had dared to break out of the family padlock, the collegiate gates, and the community fences in order to go beyond this door and enter the foremost university. God, does that sounds great! Now she must walk proudly and provocatively in keeping with the mood of her deed.

At last! Left behind are those gaudy reproductions of Marc Chagall that hang all over the living and dining room walls. Where does Father get this obsession for buying any trinket that imitates the painter? Must be his small-town taste; like all hicks, he mistakes junk for real art. Real art is these stained glass windows which, on this particular morning, shed a special light, bringing them into harmony with the modern architecture all around it. What beauty! A splendid open gallery offers her famous muralists, painters, and sculptors in quantities that go far beyond her artistic appreciation, yet is a most fitting place in which to experience this radical moment dividing her existence.

And the school building? Is it really this two-storied gray box? It looks more like a convent. What cold and penumbral classrooms! Ah, but behind the building, what a glorious field of furry green grass! Why are the walls so bare? No color, not even a line. In fact, nothing hints at the presence of young bright students everywhere.

"They put us up here in this dorm run by nuns, but it's only temporary," explains Cristina Doglio.

The animated voices of the freshmen break the still silence:

"Hey, what's up?"

"Schedule's out . . ."

"Who's teaching philosophy?"

"We get to choose from English, Italian, French, and German!"

"Wow! Look at the syllabus for Intro to Literature. That's a lot of work."

Yes, it's a new and exciting pleasure. Left behind is the daily, cloistered existence of her home in San Leopoldino. Here is an open universe without walls, so varied, it offers itself unconditionally to her every wish. No wonder the school motto is "This lighthouse is here to conquer darkness." ❖

Oy gottenyu! When will I finally be able to leave Lendov? From afar I see Pinchas Gros, the only one of us who lives among the Gentiles and in the very center of town. He's a common man who doesn't even know how to write his name and celebrates the Sabbath alone. I must admit he sure has a great talent for fixing watches and glasses. So why does he live alone? And with a big goat in his backyard? They even use him to threaten children and sinners; after all, who could bear being locked up with that enormous beast and all the noise he makes?

I still have to cross the worn-out wooden bridge where young lovers walk arm in arm, until around midnight, when Don Josú lets loose his dogs and the lovers rush back to the drugstore. From the street, the lovers look through the open window and enjoy the concert.—Oh, I forgot to tell you, the drugstore houses the only piano in town, a treasure which none of us ever really saw, but guessed was there. We all managed, at some point, to hear its notes. Standing in front of the colored containers of the drugstore, each heard a different melody. Know what I mean? Only the town priest could enter that house of enchantment. Dressed in priestly garb, he used to go very often to the house with the piano. What did the priest do there? Was he by any chance a privileged cherub? Tell you the truth, I always thought that what interested him was the pharmacist's wife. . . . And now where do I hide? Out of Guitzer Street comes Batcha and her crude husband, that chicken guzzler. Oy veis meir! That's all I need! Bitter as bile that woman is. Why, she'd cut off my hand with her kitchen knife if she so much as suspected that I had said they're not among the best of families. Save me, sweet god! And please don't let the lovers of the mill see me either. . . . Ay, ay! One night, I too, dreamt of love while caressing Janala's blond braid, inhaling her clean dress, her knotted kerchief, and her bare lips! From that intimacy at the mill, thank god, not one was ever left pregnant, god forgive! . . .

Farewell, Pappinyu and Mommala! May no evil ever befall you. Without saying good-bye, without hugs or kisses, your son goes away but does not leave you. . . .

She got rid of them. She never felt they were real men anyway. Little Jacobs, Moisheles, young Reubens. Always together since primary school. No comparison to these university hunks! Those others were sexless siblings. Angels and seraphs. Soulmates. Was any of them ever like these guys here? Machos with their meaningful glances and provocative gestures? That one over there, for instance, he could be in a Hollywood movie. He's got a Gregory Peck air about him! Ah! and the one next to him! Wow! He's the spitting image of Victor Mature! And what about that hunk of a professor? Exactly like Jorge Negrete! Slim, dark, elegant mustache, reminds me of my Charro singing:

Allá en el Rancho Grande allá donde viv-ií-a
Había una ranch-er-iita que alegre me deci-aa
Que alegre me deci-aaaaaaa

Back there in the big raa-anch, back there where I once liiii-i-ved
There was a rancherita who joyfully would saaaaaa-ay
Who joyfully would saaaaa-ay. . . .

All this guy needs is a pistol and a big sombrero! My Mexican Charro's got nothing on him. . . .

Ahhh, those matinee movies at the Rex and the afternoon ones at the Anuaco! Great but lasted barely ninety minutes whereas university life will be four years of handsome men parading deliciously before her. Farewell my old-fashioned parents! At last I'm a free little bird! ❖

Some hours earlier, during the pause between afternoon and evening prayers, as I counted the minutes, anguished by my upcoming departure, our humble house of god was a boiling caldron. The faithful were gathering in small circles, as if they were still at their market stalls. They were busy arguing: How many had actually died in the Great War? How many had we lost when General Pilsudski repelled the Russian army at the battle of Vistula?

"We should not have participated. That was a big imperialist war and some of our people sympathized with the Bolsheviks."

"That's nonsense! Didn't we give the Polish legions a Henry Barwinski?"

"Yes, we did, so what? They paid us well for that one, didn't they, idiot?"

"Did you already forget that we were accused shortly after, and still to this very day, of spying for the Russians? Have they quit calling us rightists and anti-Polish?"

"You're the one who's an idiot. You don't even know that the Polish parliament protested that falsehood."

"Nu, so it protested, so? Did anything change? Why? Why do we have to serve in an army where we are always watched and never trusted?"

"Friends, friends. Don't insult each other, please, it's Shabbos!"

"I believe that nothing about this country should be far from our concerns."

"C'mon, we've been here for centuries and we're now citizens of the Polish Republic."

"Any alternatives, stupid? There is maybe somewhere else for us to go to?"

"Maybe."

"Yeah, sure."

"Nu, you stay here then. You'd rather put up with the slaughter of your brothers, the burning of your miserable little houses, and the fact that your sons will never be able to study in a Polish school than suffer a little hunger in the Holy Land or even over there in America. Yes, gentlemen, and in exchange for all the advantages you enjoy here, you have to give your blood to their wars! We're citizens, right? That's what you're saying, right? Sure . . . You poor misguided souls."

"Can you suggest a better place? Can you? Then let's leave right away!"

"There must be some place on the face of this earth where there are no swords or Cossacks or savage thieves. . . ."

Their yarmulkes seem about to explode with all the shouting and shoving and even hitting at times, believe me! But the cantor's deep and tender voice calls them back to prayer marking the end of the Sabbath and once again, they turn meek before the splendor of the supplication. I, on the other hand, without arguing, am leaving: Momma, Poppa, I really don't want to be either hero or martyr on the Polish battlefield or anybody else's for that matter. I want to live and die my life for me. . . .

One afternoon, two months later, the students crowded together in the corridors to surround a bald young man with deep green eyes. At the same time, another one, thin, but with a noble expression on his face, is taken upstairs.

The group drowns them in hugs and tears. Even Professor Miguel Rosbaum, always isolated in his cubicle and covered in book dust, runs to embrace them. And Father Hernando, one of the most reserved students, talks on and on as never before.

"Who are they, Father Cornejo?"

"Famous people."

"From TV? movies?"

"The resistance. They're survivors. . . ."

"And what are they doing here?"

"Jesus, girl, are you Venezuelan?"

"Yes, by birth, and you?"

"Well, I was born in Spain but I, for one, know that the UN protested the exile of these young people. Also, that General Tarugo—what am I saying?—Marcos Pérez Jiménez, the president himself, was forced to grant them visas even though one is an active member of the Communist Party and the other of Democratic Action Party. But, I've already said too much, my child. Around here, by God, even the walls have ears."

For seventeen years she had been insulated from her surroundings. Who among her people took part in those passionate struggles for freedom, liberty, the sorrow of exile and jail, the excitement of a hastily called meeting against the dictator? Being a real citizen meant finding refuge for the democratic activists: distributing food and books to the opposition, whatever sublime task she might be entrusted with. Such a noble cause justified the total giving of oneself and she would eagerly sacrifice herself for this Venezuela of hers.

Dad and Mom didn't have to find out. Why should they? What good would it do? Voluntarily isolated, they would die of worry if they knew. It was too late for them to accept the demands of a new life. How could these ignorant Polish peasants ever understand, these peasants whose work week is a universe limited to a taxi route—from Plaza La Rueda to the corner of Carmelitas—from shop to home and vice versa? How could they possibly understand? ❖

Dear Poppa and Momma,

I ask you: If the Polish Gentiles win all the wars they start and will start, what do I ever gain? Quite the opposite. I'm neither Catholic, Ukrainian, Communist, or even Lithuanian. I'll always be the loser because I am who I am. That's why I'm saying good-bye. So long, really. I'm leaving but am not abandoning you. And, anyway, I remain a fervent Pole in one thing: I worry a lot about the Germans. . . .

Only yesterday Pappinyu brought home from shul a guest. This one was even poorer than us! But to share Shabbat even with only a piece of onion and herring, water instead of wine, bringing a beggar to the table, is the opportunity god grants us to praise him. No one should go hungry on his day of rest.

The paternal words proclaim the arrival of my very last Shabbat at home.

"My friend, have you ever studied?"

"Mr. David, he whose name I'm not worthy of mentioning, gave me life to go to school when I was very little, even though my clothes were patched and torn."

"How lucky, my friend! Everyone: wash your hands and let's begin the blessings!"

I envy Poppa's voice, which becomes even more beautiful during the prayer:

> *And there was afternoon and there was morning. Sixth day. And heaven and earth were created and all that they contain. And having concluded His creation on the seventh, He rested and sanctified it because on that day He concluded his work. Blessed art thou, oh Eternal God, King of the Universe, who doth create the fruit of the vine. Blessed art thou, Our Lord God, King of the world, who sanctified us and graced us with Your precepts and granted us the Sabbath to sanctify the memory of Your labor of creation. . . .*

As the prayer concludes we raise our glasses:

"Let us drink to life and for peace! L'chaim! Dear guest, make yourself at home. Tell me, if you know how to study you're already rich, don't you agree?"

"Thank you. Yes, but dear family, you also should know that poverty sticks to your skin and is hard to get rid of. It clouds wisdom. . . . I did study some, but one has to live. . . ."

"Excuse me, but poverty is no dishonor. . . ."

"Maybe not, Rebbe David, but it can make you do bad things. . . ."

"Yes, but I believe those bad deeds can be erased with the mortar of good deeds."

"You really think so? I think that wherever you go, wherever you stop, poverty is always in the middle of everything. That's what I think."

"Will you do me the honor of eating this gefilte fish? And tell me, my friend, did you ever try to overcome it by working with a paintbrush or with a needle and thread?"

"One has to learn many things, Sir, and, no cloak is big enough to hide poverty."

"Nu, so how do you manage?"

"I manage. . . ."

A candelabra with two candles barely sheds enough light upon us, but the vast darkness is illuminated by Poppa's every sentence and the amusing answers of Haim Lisrak, our guest who is poorer than us.

Meanwhile, Momma and my siblings doze off exhausted. Since sunrise they've been throwing sawdust on the floor trying to get it to shine, rubbing out ashes, fetching water at the well, grinding and seasoning fish, getting dressed, blessing the candles. . . . Yes, Shabbos relaxes the spirit but sure tires the body!

"Have another drink, dear guest. It's cherry brandy. A little wine lightens the heart. May you never be poor of soul. May your children grow to study Torah, to marry and to do good deeds! L'chaim! As long as there is health. . . ."

"You know, Rebbe David, poverty is worse than fifty plagues combined."

"But god only hates the ignorant. . . ."

"That may be so, but there is no crueler joke of divine affection that an empty pocket!"

"Listen, Haim, even the poorest beggar with pants full of holes, with seven different coats and seven masks to go begging alms from the same rich man, can enjoy the honor of Shabbat."

"Tsk, tsk, tsk! I certainly won't argue with that, Rebbe. That's why I keep praying: Help me, god, send me the cure, I already have the ailment!"

Outside my whole village is a single chant to god. Aromas of hot cabbage soup seeping into every corner. I don't remember when I decide to put an end to the dialogue. Anyway, if people who have read Scripture and have eaten at the same table don't exchange words on Holy Laws, they might as well kneel before an idol. Besides, these two have already argued enough. Before the prayer of thanksgiving for the food we had just received, I interrupt with a not very sacred matter: I ask Poppa to use his formidable influence to have the district bureaucrats fix the public baths. "Oy yoy yoy, my poor nose, Pappinyu! Phew! I've got to cover it tightly before I can even go in to empty out the waste containers. And you know what all the gossips say? That right next to the women's ritual baths, young ladies become pregnant! Seems that the very learned, who sing sublime harmonies and sway as they extol the glories of our lord, every night of the week, are actually reading passionate love letters that pretty young girls hand them, while emptying the leftovers into that smelly hovel . . . deep below this mystical village. . . . Poppa . . ."

Was there ever a Sunday without guests at home? First in the house in San José and then the one in San Leopoldino. Any writer, speaker, delegate, or visitor who passed through Caracas was compelled to be a dinner guest in the small and modest apartment in the Edificio de Nuestra Señora del Carmen. A pretty incongruous name for a building that housed people with unusual traditions like ours, and which many a guest had ironically pointed out to their hosts. We lived there since the time Father almost went bankrupt. It was a place full of books, magazines, and phony Chagalls. Its only luxury was an Erard piano reflected in the glass cabinet full of crystal objects. These had been gifts from the Landaus, the Sponkas, the Erders, and others, when they moved into the lovely house on the same street eight years later, the house that had to be sold in a hurry to avoid foreclosure.

Today's luncheon is one of many. This one is given for the writer Isaiah Rainfeld. As usual, Don Máximo had already taken and brought him back from the business area of town: "Because one must try to distribute the books of this known intellectual however one can. Whether those buyers read the hardbound volumes or just use them to decorate their libraries is irrelevant. It's a fundamental act of charity to help a wise man. Besides, we'll need real dollars to pay for the American edition of poems of resistance in the ghettoes.

During the week, the business on Pasaje Benzo between Madrices and Marrón streets was in the capable hands of the missus. After all, isn't she the expert in buying and selling bras, half-slips, and panties? Her husband? Oh he's something else! Culture on agile legs and convincing lips. Yeah, a regular walking encyclopedia. No denying that.

"We sold thirty-six books, Mr. Rainfeld."

"That's great, my friend."

"In three more days, we'll sell all seventy. We'll go to the big tycoons secluded in their enormous mansions."

"It seems to be easier to write books than to sell them, don't you think?"

"Nonsense. Relax. Nobody ever turns me down. No matter where I knock, you saw that yourself. They know that I have never traded with someone else's gold. I am not a smuggler. I don't charge a cent of commission for the sacred labor of helping the learned. Just as I learned from my father David, may he have found peace. . . ."

The exquisite banquet the lady of the house prepared, almost at daybreak, overflows on platters. Gefilte fish, chicken soup and matzoh balls, nuts, cakes, grapes. The best of the best. "One must always honor the intellect!"

And now, the moment of truth has arrived. Could there be a better setting to bring up the issue of her great leap?

"Father, tomorrow I'm beginning my studies at the university. . . ."

"This isn't the moment to discuss . . ."

"I'm not discussing, I'm notifying."

"Tonight when there are no guests, we'll talk. . . ."

"Why wait? I already registered and in fact, I'm also going to be teaching at the Colegio Canada."

"I'm embarrassed in front of Mr. Rainfeld, he understands Spanish . . . you're so obstinate. . . ."

"That's a fact."

"A daughter of mine? Practically engaged? Should get involved in that dangerous place where Reds hide and the National Security guards go looking for them with guns? That's sacrilege! Please, Mr. Rainfeld, honored guest, excuse us and help yourself to more fish."

Nothing better to dissolve her anger at Father than the Louie Armstrong open air concert at the Concha Acústica de Bello Monte brought from heaven itself just for her! Instead of screams, the sensual poetry of Gershwin's Summerti-i-me and the living is e-ea-sy. . . . ❖

Over there in Lendov, how many strangers had Friday and Saturday meals at my parents' humble table? Impossible to count. Occasionally, the guest might even be a modern freethinker from the city.

"But, Mr. David, Charles Darwin already proved that man is just another animal. . . ."

"What are you saying, young man? If that's so, then how come not a single animal ever produced a Darwinich, or whatever his name is?"

"Rebbe, he's an English naturalist who, after observing the animal species, determined their degree of evolution. . . . No, sorry, nothing to do with our God."

"If a horse had something to say he would speak. . . ."

"That's not what we're discussing, Mr. David. Beasts have their own way of expressing themselves."

"Yes, yes, they have tongues, that's true, but they cannot say a single blessing!"

"They express themselves in sounds and gestures."

"Young man, the ignorant is not the one who does not know, but the one who scorns divine knowledge. And don't you forget that! A goat has a beard but that doesn't make it a priest. Does it?"

"Ah! Finally we agree on something. Sir, you do admit then that we are the higher ranked in the animal kingdom?"

"You said that, I didn't. Anyway, before you become too big for your own breeches, young man, remember that butterflies precede *you* in the kingdom of divine creation! . . ."

And so they might continue until the moon descended and the sun dazzled us. . . .

Ahhhh! Her intoxication continues with the music of Jelly Roll Morton. . . . The mixture of sweet wine and wrathful words at the end of Mr. Isaiah Rainfeld's reception fueled her tenacious will to face her opponent and pursue the confrontation:

"Father, I beg you! Please try to understand my wish to have a career."

"I understand and cannot tie you to the house, or prohibit you from having an honorable profession. Quite the opposite, I want you to amount to something, not be like me, who never got a diploma, who could not study and so had to earn a living knocking on doors, peddling, selling schmates. What do you want from me, Kindele? I'm afraid for you! In that political environment of atheists!"

"But, Dad, you're not even religious!"

"Yes, I most certainly am, in my own way. It's true I no longer pray everyday and I don't do a full fast on Yom Kippur and no doubt because of that my Poppa is turning in his grave. But, I practice my tradition every moment of my life. And, as you well know, I've made a sacred cult of my mother-tongue, Yiddish. Have you ever known me to sleep away from home, even one night? Do I have children on the streets? Do I get drunk? Gamble? Other women? That's what you're going to be exposed to out there. I'm afraid for you and for your sisters. . . ."

"Please, please, try to understand. We can't stay locked up forever. Each of us has to forge her own life! You did it, or have you already forgotten? You broke with your family and crossed oceans!"

"That was very different, young lady! Don't confuse the issues! I stayed back in Lendov, just my feet left! Can you understand that?"

"No, not at all. Anyway, why not just pretend that I'm not leaving San Leopoldino either, just my beautiful legs are running in search of other roads?"

A seemingly never-ending dialogue was being repeated, but she decided that as of this night it was ending. Max's moist eyes and Rifka's long sad face, marked with silent resentment, her leave taking at breakfast.

Would it have been wiser to go to another country? With what money? Maybe she just lacked the courage to cut, really cut that heavy chord. . . . ❖

As I was telling you, at the end of Shabbat, I'm leaving, without a word. I have a foreboding that I'm saying good-bye forever to Nune the carpenter, Toiba the cripple, and Leib the hunchback. Oy gottenyu, how deeply my heart aches for Momma, the blanket that covers all my weaknesses.

And when at last, Lendov is behind me, I jump, practically fly to Magelnitze without spending even a minute in that ugly little town where I used to come so often to buy yarmulkes. Its very smell upsets me. You see, when someone from my village closes their eyes forever, he is wrapped in his tallis, covered in straw, and then sent in a carriage to this overcrowded cemetery. Its stench freezes my bones!

"Magelnitze is sacred because it's where the eternal house is," my father used to say. "It's the good place," my mother usually added. You know what I think? I think it's the only place in the entire world where someone from our village has a right to his own little piece of land! That's what I think. And anyway, this business of putting the dead in face down, boy, that really buries a person! Even if they swear to me that it's the real garden of Eden, and it's where all the dead will be resurrected, I still prefer gardens that are above and not below ground. Above, always above. You know what I mean? Even with all the hunger, plagues, pogroms. Nu, what can I tell you?

I don't stop at Vialorovsker either, because I know for sure that one-eyed Zina lurks right behind that window. Poor girl, she's been waiting for me to become engaged to her for four or five years now. . . .

I point my face to heaven and cross the main road like a thunderbolt. I couldn't bear to feel her rancorous gaze.

"Get married? But Poppa, I'm just fifteen years old!"

"So what? I got married at the same age and I'm just fine, no?"

"But that's not good enough for me. From a cat a scratch; from a child bride nothing but damnation."

"What are you saying, my boychick? To get up early and marry early never hurt anyone. You'll have a good dowry and time to study Scripture."

"Pappinyu, you know why the bear dances? Because he has no wife. Give him one and he'll stop dancing. They sing that one at the market, Poppa."

"But it's a lie, because a husband is like a king and all couples are fine after a year or so."

"No, no, and no. It's never too late to marry or to die, Pappinyu."

"Oy veis meir! May the one whose name is blessed forgive your affront, my son! You're very stubborn and I worry night and day about how you'll end up."

And while he wails, pulling hairs out of his long black beard, I run away to help Momma with the town fair where she buys us used clothes. . . .

That whole week was full of tension and whispers. Finally, on Friday night, when the rest of the family sleeps, he speaks. He looks worried.

"Where does one begin such unpleasant business? My dear sweet daughter, I want to consult you on a very delicate matter." In a low voice: "Please don't get upset. But ah . . . Manuel Rabinovich, the engineer, destined to be your husband, and from such a good family too, grandson of wise people! Well, anyway, he asked for a dowry, a house, car, office, and if possible, some cash. . . ."

The father, knowing full well his daughter's wickedly complicated personality, has to tell her the whole truth. . . . Should he get a bank loan? What does she think?

"Well, I'm not surprised. It is customary, after all. The problem is I still like him even after six months. Elegant, handsome, first kiss and out together, in a group, of course, to places like that fabulous Montmartre in Baruta with its European music and the naughty Pasapoga with its mambos and guarachas."

"Thanks for the warning, Dad. If I were you, I wouldn't do anything." Of course in historical terms, a dowry was after all a justifiable institution even under a Marxist focus . . . but it had nothing to do with love. "Tell me, Dad, how much did you make when you married?"

"Your mother with three cotton dresses. . . ."

"Well, that's just about what I think you should fork over. . . ."

At times, Max could seem primitive and abrupt in his reactions, but he had never been a good peddler. He was unable to sell his daughter. His smile, overflowing with impishness, signed a pact of complicity. On that point at least, there was never any argument. ❖

It's a long way to Warsaw. And to be honest, it was none too sweet. But then again, I guess it could have been worse. On the way to Prztyk and Gora Kalwaria, I befriended a couple of coachmen. I've heard it said that god should protect us from forced exile and from coachmen, but, even though these were pretty rough guys, I could tell they weren't totally stupid. Look, these unfortunate men travel for so long facing their horses, after a while they themselves become like animals.

Anyway, I really liked Nisale, the frisky one. After listening to all my Oy yoy yoyings over my calf pains, one afternoon he asked me: "Tell me, young sir, you seem quite learned, what do we really need our legs for? After all, to Hebrew school we are taken, to our wedding we are driven, to our grave we are carried, to the temple we never go, and in front of all pretty Gentile girls we prostrate ourselves. . . . So, what do you think, do we need them for anything?"

"Yes, Nisale. We need them to take us to America the Golden!"

He remained pensive. Probably not half as old as he looked with those smooth toothless gums. I took great care to keep to myself, my ideas about the feet being the very center of a penitent's soul. Like Joel, the bearded one dressed in rags, who showed up one day at my village. "May his body be feverish for nine years!" "A pox on him!" "He should only grow like an onion, with his head buried in the ground!" they all cursed him. Only a few of the women gave him some stale bread and water, moved by his misfortune.

To make a long story short, Momma, teary eyed, tells me about the great Joel, born in the big city of Vilna, whose voice, at thirteen, was already legendary throughout the country. He sang the prayers with the virtuosity of the chosen. One day a famous Gentile composer hears him at an event and, overwhelmed, begs the parents to allow him to be the child's teacher. Years later, while in the capital singing profane tunes, Joel meets Katiuska, a Polish princess. They fall madly in love. So at the age of twenty-two, Joel abandons his singing career and, rejected by his people, he who had been so pious and devout decides to atone for his sins. He goes from village to village dragging himself to each and every little broken down house until he gets to ours. What grief his broken down body bears! And even you two, my very own parents, watch him suspiciously between the slits of the window shutters.

Dear parents, in this letter I can finally tell you that as I felt his child-like face and white hair wandering feverishly around the alleys of my childhood, I was more frightened than I had ever been in my life. A leper without sores.

I was reminded of the story of the king and the two men who guarded his orchard: one blind and one cripple:

"I see some delicious ripe fruit but I can't reach it with only one leg," says the cripple.

"So what do you need two legs for? If you stand on my shoulders, we'll both eat juicy apples. I don't need eyes to taste them. Why should you need two legs?" And that's exactly what they did. When the king found out, he questioned his guards.

"Your Highness, how could it have been me? I can't climb or walk."

"Do you believe, your Worship, that I could have picked them without seeing?"

The king ordered the cripple to get on the shoulders of the blind man and then sentenced both to die.

Body and soul must always go together, Poppa. I have finally realized that if succumbing to pleasure sickens one's head, then one ends up with pain like Joel's and in an asylum in Warsaw. I will never be a cantor like my brother, nor a Moil like you, Pappinyu, much less one of those chosen to study god's words fifteen hours a day. Now and with this letter, I can finally tell you one of the reasons I left home without kissing you good-bye. Please try to understand. Just like you can't dance at two weddings at the same time, I don't want to separate my heart from my head. Poppa, Momma, dear little brothers and sisters, please don't cry when you think of me. . . .

"That's what we need our feet for, Nisale, to save ourselves in America. . . ."

No puedo ser feliz
No te puedo olvidar
Siento que te perdí
Y eso me hace pensar
Que he renunciado a ti
Ardiente de pasión
No se puede tener
consciencia y corazón

I cannot be happy
I cannot forget you
I feel I've lost you
And that makes me think
I've given you up
Burning with passion
It's impossible to have a conscience and a heart.

Love sickness. Ahhhh, the main event in all the big fat novels, but never a personal calamity. Certainly not for one who, sick in bed with measles, impassively devoured boxes and boxes of chocolates while the novel's heroines—the Lady of the Camellias and María the consumptive—were dying.

Suffering a respiratory illness in response to an existential crisis was the classic doctoral dissertation for all literature majors ever since Hans Castorp had been interned in the Magic Mountain's hospital. It was also Thomas Mann's pretext for surgically examining how the cream of European culture hatched the fascist serpent's egg, and other issues, from that distant mountain. It was quite a different thing, and pretty devastating at that, to suffer from wounded self-love and worse still, to choke on held-back tears over: asthma.

The choice between wishing and thinking was no longer that melodramatic vulgarity she had enjoyed so much while getting over many a childhood illness. Since the beginning of time, for instance, it was normal to consider milking cows as a valuable object of barter. And that give-and-take seems not to have offended anyone. Now, with her lungs crushed, she wondered: Would it ever come to that for her? Would they have to barter this woman, lover, companion, person? . . . They say that Eichmann bartered trucks and tanks for bunches of us, undesirable to his Aryan race . . . and . . . I can't breathe! . . . I need air!

A reddish eruption covers her pores. Each little oozing blister is an unscreamed scream, an unspit spit, an unvomited insult. . . .

Ya no estás más a mi la-do, co-ra-zón
Y en el alma sólo tengo so-le-dad
Y si ya no puedo ve-erte
¿Por qué Dios me hizo que-rer-te?
Para hacerme sufrir má-as. . . .

You're no longer at my side, my darling love
And there is nothing but sadness in my heart
And I can no longer see you
Why did God make me love you
Just to see me suffer so-oooo.

What would dejection be without this romantic duet by Lucho Gatica repeated ad nauseum on the General Electric record player, which really should be turned in for one of those newer automatic ones.

Es la historia de un a-mo-or
Como no hay otro i-gua-al
Que me hizo compren-de-er
Todo bien
Todo mal.
Que le dio luz a mi vi-i-da

It's the story of a lo-ove
Like no other before

That allowed me to se-ee
All that's good
All that's bad
That brought light into my li-iife. . . .

Forget the verses of Lamartine, or Alfonsina Storni, forget Neruda's poems of Love and La Canción Desesperada. None helped as much as those wise boleros which so languidly admit the pain and allow you to cry your eyes out. . . . Oh that feels sooo good!

Mouth, sex, fingers, and ears have turned into horrendous blisters. Didn't do much for her looks. No danger in being taken for Elizabeth Taylor! No, not even Doris Day! "Doctor, please, can this sickly fragility of hers lead to frigidity? What about emotional coldness?" She cried on and on. . . . He's got a lot of other beautiful and rich girlfriends. And, what about her? Things will work out, eventually. She'll just have to look harder. . . . "You know, asthma's the chronic illness of idealists," her allergy doctor tells her while giving her yet another shot. ❖

"Mr. Joel Stransky? Oh yes. I'm sorry, he died last spring. Yes, right here in the sanatorium."

"Oy! May his soul have found peace! It hurts me deeply, mister director. Before leaving for America I wanted to come to Warsaw to give Joel this because when he passed through our village, the only charity we could give him was a little food. We're so poor ourselves, you see, that nobody had a full suit to give him. Anyway, now that I'm leaving Poland, and I'll not be needing this prayer shawl for a long time, I wanted him to have it. Oy yoy yoy! I walked so much! I went so far out of my way, and still, you see, I'm too late!"

"Mr. Joel died of insanity, you know?"

Of love, I say to myself. Once again, curses arrive faster than telegrams! And my efforts were as successful as those of three deaf old women running a music school. . . .

That whole day was nocturnal. I had run up and down the avenues of this great capital for two days and their nights, dozing here and there for a few hours in parks, always asking for Joel the Cantor. Finally, on Sienna Street I saw some of our people going in and out of a house. . . . Yes, Number 18, I remember. . . . From the open door I saw a children's puppet show. Standing there, weak from hunger, lack of sleep, and mourning, who should I bump into? None other than Nathan the Orphan, who had left Lendov years ago! While he asks about all his neighbors, he keeps pinching me to make sure it's really me and not a vision. . . .

Nathan is the doorman at the asylum run by Doctor Korczac who sheltered him from the time he ran away from our village. He talks and talks while leading me to Number 92 Krochmalna Street. There, he leaves me at the door while he goes to check with Miss Stephanie, the doctor's assistant, to see if they can shelter me for a few days. "Yes, brother. You can stay and rest in a little bed in the back corner of the common bedroom."

There I will dream of warm arms protecting me, just as those children are protected by Doctor Crazy. Can you believe that's what the Poles called him, crazy? I know they say that if somebody yells out "crazy" you should watch your step carefully, but I can assure you that in this case they were very wrong. Maestro Janusz, which is what his adopted children called him, slept in that enormous room and on a decrepit bed, just like and together with his little orphans. His appearance was that of a Holy Man. Very skinny, pointy beard, always with an impeccably clean white robe. He wore it night and day and it also served him as blanket on those cold Warsaw nights. Once recovered, on the fourth day, I decided to try to earn a few cents for my trip. Nathan spoke to his comrade Gerson, a ticket taker at the theater. He lent me the right to his job for one performance. Half the proceeds of the Kaminska Company performance! And let me tell you, that night I earned a lot more than I bargained for. And not just in money, either. Right then and there, the very minute I saw her, I fell madly in love for the very first time in my life. A man's love. . . .

When all the tickets are taken I decide to watch the show. Ida Kaminska is a gypsy called Esmeralda, and the director is Turkow, her husband. The audience, all dressed up in their Sunday best, applauded frenetically every time Esmeralda/Ida spoke. Her picture on the program's cover accompanies me all the way to Germany, where it got wet in the Oder River. But that's another story and it comes later. . . .

How can I describe how much I cried during the performance watching Quasimodo's suffering? I think that was the name of that hunchback from Paris. A deaf bellringer, ugly but good, a generous soul, called mockingly the King of the Dumb. I felt like him, a deformed dwarf, mistreated in my loneliness in Warsaw by this new hidden love for Esmeralda, the dancer who gave me pity and a new energy just when I needed it most.

That night, at the orphanage, Ida was mine. And when I awake I don't feel the slightest bit guilty. You know why? Easy. In our sleep we don't really sin. Only our dreams do! I am still as innocent as a newborn babe. . . .

The fall of a dictator liberates even those who did not suffer his chains. The crowds celebrate their freedom after ten harsh years of tyranny. For her, freedom was her hot blood running wild, surging through all her veins at once with ferocious energy.

Instead of a lecture on Greek theater, a secret date! Ah, as exciting as any of those delicious French films at the Palace Theater. Oh la la! Gerard Philippe and Jean Gabin, sometimes the treacherous charm of Maurice Chevalier. And always, always Yves, divine Montand. . . . How come this urge for an often married Gentile with no money?

Reloj no marques las ho-ras
Porque voy a enloquece-er . . .
El se me irá para siempre
Cuando amanezca-a otra ve-ez
Detén el tiempo en tus ma-a-nos
Haz esta noche per-pe-tua

Dear clock please don't strike the hours,
For I will go ma-ad
He will leave me for-e-ver
When the da-w-nn arri-i-ves. . . .

Later, guilt, more guilt, and discouragement: Why this mania for another helping of rejection? "What do you doctors call that anxiety that accelerates the pulse and almost suffocates? Sin without seduction or tenderness? Sort of like vengeance by shock, no?"

Gone are the days filled with moments of clandestine little revenges. She'll try to fill some of the emptiness with a bibliography of the Spanish spoken in the Americas and anyway, final exams are practically here. But her anaemic state still requires an occasional sensual bolero. . . .

The old folks would be relieved if they only knew that their rebellious, marriageable young lady plays with fire but has not yielded. Proof? Hymen's still intact! Isn't that the unequivocal test of virginity? Seems the black sheep of the family is a little wild, but, still chaste. . . . ❖

What I loved about Warsaw was that on every street there was a theater, as if it were a necessary electric street light. Before leaving for America, I had time to go with Nathan to the Public Theater and from the very last row enjoy the performance of the Khane Grosberg Band. The next morning we were still laughing at their jokes.

But my life's not up to joking. I had a set plan and already seven days have passed. Winter is coming and I have only one change of clothes. It has to be now! Yes! I must hurry! Someday soon, I'll come back and settle down right here. Then I'll sit just like a big shot, accustomed to the cafes of the big world, and you, Beautiful Warsaw, will entertain me with recitals, bookreadings, and musical evenings. See you soon!

I can go two ways. If I go to the immigration center, they'll send me to Gdansk. In that case, I won't be allowed to choose where in America I want to go to. . . . I wonder why they call Gdansk a free port; it's just the opposite, really. They actually decide for you where you're going. So I risk it and go west to Berlin, with no papers. It's a long journey. I survive on spoiled herring, dried turnips, and bitter cigarette stubs. But all the hunger I suffer is worth what my eyes are discovering: the meaning of a beautiful landscape! I'm like a newborn at twenty! Can you understand my excitement?

Sknierniewice, Brzeziny, Lodz, Kalisz, Sbaszyn, not to mention all the little towns in between, offer themselves to me among forests of beech trees, woods of unbelievably tall oaks, the clean smell of pines, waterfalls that sound like human voices. Nu? So who needs food?

Salme Goldstein, barefooted and dexterous in the handling of his vegetable cart, is not one of those idiots easily amazed that a flea has a belly button, no, sir. Within sight of immense towers with red and white flags, he looks deep into my eyes: "My son," he says, "that's the fortress of the Duke of Petrovski. In Count Bucovich's mansion over there, you could see everything that was ever in Noah's Ark. Take my word for it. He's got deer, otters, wolves, bears, you name it. See, what they do with their money is buy everything on god's good earth. They've never tasted *our* cabbage soup. They have only the finest victuals of exquisite meat on gold and silver platters, stuffed potatoes, nuts of all kinds, and even whiskey to drink. On the other hand, my son, if you've ever seen one of us eat chicken it's because either the chicken or one of us is sick.

Salme's sonorous voice telling me about other people's wealth takes me back in time. I'm at the wedding of Count Kuzinski's daughter, many years back, when they requested that musicians from my village play at the celebration. I, the youngest in the orchestra, with my mandolin, Rubin on violin, Sholem on trumpet, Jacob on the contrabass, and Jonah on the drums were taken by servants to the castle near Kielce, many, many miles from home. It was exhausting, but it allowed us to make a few kopeks to give to Momma for a little yellow chicken soup, which cures colds and gets rid of pains, you know. And, most special of all, for a little fresh fish for the Sabbath!

I myself was already putting away a little something for my escape, which I hoped would take place as soon as I was old enough. You know? Maybe that's why god punished me, because while we were bathing in a river, learning to swim, someone stole all my money!

Anyway, we were on our way to the wedding wearing shiny black shoes which miraculously became bigger with every passing year and still fit us! Nu, you didn't know that a poor boy's shoes grow with his feet? We wore white socks which got shorter and shorter every day, black knee-length pants, long dress coats, and top hats. Nu? So it's summer and we're boiling hot. So? Never mind. That's how we had to dress. Some of us already had a little beard and all had curly locks around our ears. To tell you the truth, when I dressed like that, I used to think that I was masquerading for Queen Esther's party even though I knew that Purim was in March, before Pesach.

During the wedding feast, the Christians, seated on red brocaded chairs, listen to polkas and mazurkas. Later, they go out on the terraces and as drunk as Lot, dance to Ukrainian, Hungarian, and even our Yiddish melodies which we play very well. By now they are stuffed with pig and gravy, and liquors which we never get to taste because even though the partying lasts four days, we bring our own little packages of toasted wheat from home, grabbing a pear or orange here and there.

Yes, we are different. But, I'll tell you a secret. Though I want neither their honey nor their sting, I feel a little sorry for the Poles of nobility who have to rent our joy.

While they dance, I remember a tale my brother Isrul Hersh, the quiet musical one once told me. He was driving rich Count Casimir Rupnovsky, the one who always wore a wide military sash around his waist, and who owned all the lands around Lendov. Anyway, moved by Hershele's beautiful voice singing local songs, the old Pole became tearful: "You know, my son, our grandparents and great-grandparents were attacked by Germans and Cossacks and Turks and Tartars and Swedes and Russians. But centuries of killings did not manage to destroy us, and you know why?"

"I don't, Sir, I . . ."

"Well, you should! It's because we always fought, without ever giving up, in order to preserve the chain of our golden freedom!"

As I listened to the story I told my brother that all we had to do was add the murderous brutality of the Poles themselves to Count Rupnovsky's enemies' list and we'd have the complete list of our own executioners. They did not succeed in liquidating us either. "So, pay attention and learn, Hershele. We also endured blood and fire for our golden chain of tradition. But without palaces, marble statues, land under our feet, servants, or pigs. That's why you and I are rich and very noble. Understand me?"

When Salme the coachman tells me that chewing the apple one discovers the worm, a needle pierces the very center of my heart. If it's true that Field Marshal Joseph Pilsudski just led a coup to take over the government (that's what Nathan and Gerson said in Warsaw) and if he, as my friends claim, is really a Socialist, how much longer will he allow Poland to be divided between a few old lords, owners of these lands, and the millions of starving peasants who also inhabit these beautiful wheat fields? He's got a tough job because it's harder to cure an embittered heart than a cold stomach. And besides, what are we? We, far away in a deserted village, neither owners nor slaves, in the middle of everything and of nothing. *What are we?*

And I, who am I? I tremble to think that I'll enter Germany without any documents, as if I were a delinquent. I've been told that the Poles and the Germans are good friends who always fear each other. Make any sense? One thing is for sure, I'm not worried about the language. Who among us, no matter how land-loving, how common, how much of an illiterate brute he might be, who among us doesn't understand German? Our everyday language, sucked with maternal milk, is really German mixed with the language of the Sacred Scriptures, a smidgen of Russian, and a touch of Polish. . . . But let me tell you, the Germans might be a cultured people, but their language sounds so harsh that I feel incapable of speaking it. Not at all like our sweet mother tongue, Yiddish. Not at all. Nu, so somehow I'll manage to get along. As you may have noticed, I'm not exactly a mute. . . .

Far into the night, Salme stops, turns his cart, and says good-bye with a long yawn. We're here. Good-bye Poland! Good-bye? Does anyone ever really abandon the place of his childhood?

The break has been complete. . . . The narrow, asphyxiating past ended once and for all. Now there is no doubt she is someone quite different. Her language is elevated and her writing overly ornate. She expounds on Goethe and Hesse, Boll and Grass with an impressive arsenal of German idioms that amaze the very demanding Dr. Erika Lotter. Frau Professor delights in that correct pronunciation of terms and names which she says the "locals" deform beyond recognition, which, of course, bothers her deeply. It not only threatens her standing in the department but accounts for her terrible classroom outbursts.

Essays on Shakespeare and Baroja, Rubén Darío and Vallejo, Pedro Emilio Coll and Guillermo Meneses. "These works reflect a very keen critical mind," say her professors: the austere Peter Smith Stone, the kind Bompiani, and the gentle Juan Reyes Landaeta.

"What very fine use of vocabulary and syntax. You'll be a great teacher, and right here too. After all, minds like yours are exactly what we need. And such command of language! Hard to believe that your parents are European peasants!

"Come to a party on Sunday. Our kind of people will be there, know what I mean?"

"It's important for you to show up at these functions so that you get to meet the right people, the ones who'll facilitate your joining the faculty. A group of party exiles, just returned from Mexico, will be there, and you really should be seen with them."

She was treading on the sublime shores of academic sanctity and praised for her use of the language fed to her by her nurse maids: the honey-sweet, thick-lipped black one and her mustachioed dried-up Andean one who also taught her the art of radio—soap opera listening: "The Divine and Invincible Tamakún"; silly and entertaining "Tontín and Tontona"; and the hair-raising "When Destiny Calls," all on Continental Radio. Ah! and let's not forget the books: fairy tales, Brothers Grimm, the Count of Montecristo, Old and New Testament, the Three Musketeers, Wuthering Heights. Not to mention the comics that Father always bought on Sundays, when they both devote to the girls all the time that the business and charity deeds take up during the week. Six wicked days with the maids! Could that be the reason, Doctor, that one often feels something akin to terror, as if, once again, one were trespassing the forbidden limits of someone else's property?" ❖

A cave like darkness barely lit by my pupils surrounds me along the narrow stretch of the Oder River. It is pretty low around this time of year since the hot summer dried much of the river bed, as we had heard from travelers. Another reason I had to leave now, this year. I swim like a baby fish with my money sack tied to my forehead. The noisy beats of my poor terrified heart prevent the river from freezing me forever. As I step upon the opposite shore, what do I see but a committee of border guards, all smiles, all waiting for me.

I was so frightened and so cold that I fainted. When I come to at the police station, I hear loud roars. Military orders. The sounds of that language are so harsh!

Grandma Pearl used to say that you don't show a job half way done to a fool. Her advice came to mind and in broken German I said: "Hey guys, you're right, it's true I am Polish, but, I'm running away because I think they're horrible devils. Why am I running? Simple. I don't want to serve in their army. Why? Simple. I don't ever want to kill a single one of you Germans. Why? What do you mean why? Because I love the way you speak, the way you laugh, your sweet and bucolic songs, and, most of all, your delicious beer! What possible motive could I have to kill Germans in battle when you guys never did me any harm?"

"Well, then, why don't you stay here with us?"

"Gee, I'd love to but my mother is in America and I can't give her up, even for you. . . ."

If you're going to eat pork and it's going to stain your beard and chin, do it well and without guilt, I say. And so, with the same glee with which the idiot laughs because his mother bore him and not another, so these soldiers laugh while they smugly applaud my words. A sharp hunger, the kind that splits your guts, plus an incredible exhaustion completely overwhelm me and I fall into a deep sleep. I dream I arrive in New York and go up to the Statue of Liberty. I flirt with her and she, forgetting she's made of stone (or is it metal?) answers with a wink of complicity without ever lowering the torch. That's how it is, you know, we really can make our dreams more important than night itself.

The next day, right on the same chair where I had dreamt so nicely, I get greasy sausages, black bread, and pretty stale tepid tea. A blue-eyed officer hands me some papers: a passport and a French visa good for three weeks. "Schöne danken schöne danken! Many many thanks!" I ask for my money and my knapsack back. When a cheater kisses you, always count your teeth!

So ends my short honeymoon with Germany. They took me to the station in an official car. In a sweat of happiness, I left on a German train which, you, gottenyu, miraculously provided for, you of whom I am less and less worthy with each passing moment! By the way, gottenyu, let me ask you something, since you're always in my heart, why do I have to waste time looking for you in the heavens?

I'll try and tell you the next part a little faster. Between Berlin and Paris I melt with the pleasure of the views. You see, where I come from there were no hills, birds, or such beautiful flowers and certainly no such clear air. I could stay here for a hundred and twenty years and enjoy this parade of living creatures if only they'd let me! It's true what wisemen say that there are three things that soften a man's heart: a sweet melody, pleasing scenery, and a fragrant smell. I feel those blessings, god's radiance, piercing my very skin.

In my village, when someone described such countrysides, we were always sure that they were old wive's tales, inventions of vagrants to mesmerize their audience. Now I have proof that they exist and, in fact, abound. I could smell the fragrance of Paradise right here on earth. In Lendov, we refrained from these pleasures because peasants tie themselves to their prayer books and don't travel much.

But I ask you, dear god: Aren't the rigors of your laws hard enough on us? Why do we always have to add new ones of our own?

This open and varied world is mine now! Art films, museums, recitals, debates, talks, the writer Rómulo Gallegos in the auditorium, the painter Jesús Soto, the composer Antonio Estévez, the actress Juana Sujo, the director Horacio Paterson. My heavens! This country is full of wonders! Image, cadence, oil paintings, chromatic, discursive line,

Fall of the West, the Berlin Wall, Sartre, Dos Passos, Faulkner, southern borders, the Other America, Civil Rights. Pretty tight agenda! Where does one begin? Where has she been until now? How do you assimilate all without becoming intoxicated? Pop art, Cultural Revolution, Mao, Viet Nam, Marcuse, bookstore cocktail party to unveil book of poems, writers' conferences, national, continental, and international prizes. . . . Pleasant Gabriel García Márquez, handsome Mario Vargas Llosa, brilliant and deep Emir Rodríguez Monegal! And what salons! Perfect ambiance for copious whiskey consumption, cigarette smoking, and expressing oneself elegantly while letting an occasional four-letter word into the conversation. Are there any good reasons why one shouldn't enjoy these marvels of civilized living? Where exactly does the desecration lie? Why feel guilty? And anyway, desecration of what?

One thing is for certain. This excites skin and brain. So, to hell with all those No No Nos. After all, they repress impulses and sensibility. You know all about this, Doctor, and especially all about Sigmund Freud. And even though you never answer my questions, I know I'm right.

Who, and in the name of whom or what, is going to stop my right to give in to my senses? The Bible? The Talmud? The Kabala? And with what right? Where have I been all this time without joining this orgy of real culture? ❖

But, in this life, all good things come to an end, and the good a lot sooner than the bad. Arriving at the Gare de l'Est in Paris, I am petrified with fear and remain so for, I don't know, minutes? hours? No one there to meet me. I'm a wanderer without friends in a big city. When the train departs, its bellowing seems to echo my fearful worries. I remain on the platform overwhelmed. Oy gottenyu! Help me find your temple in this foreign and crowded immensity! I wander around, asking in broken German where I might find a synagogue.

I've got to put on my phylacteries and thank the Lord of the Universe for giving me health and life and getting me here. Finally, I reach Consistorio Street where I find my sanctuary. I come without a yarmulke, without tallis, with nothing. Dino Feket, the village teacher, is right when he says: "If a soldier who serves the tzar must always wear a uniform, then so should an enlisted man who serves the Almighty carry with him all the tools of his prayers."

I'm sure you understand the infinite peace I felt upon entering, don't you? Without even asking me who I am, the first thing they do is wail "Blessed he who arrives!" and they hand me the delicate black laces which I roll around my left arm until they make the initials of the word God. I cover myself in the white and blue striped prayer shawl. I kiss the strands. I cry. Once again I have a family and my spirit has been rekindled. How much, I wonder, did my sweet Momma cry following the sudden departure of her son? My Mommala is a candle. She illuminates others while she herself gets consumed. . . .

At the end of the prayer, they descended upon me with questions and hugs. "What's the news from home?" "Have they recruited many for the service?" "Is there any way to make a living?"

You might not believe this, but I felt as if I were in Lendov even though I'd never seen any of these people before. Dressed in gabardine pants, with fancy ties, suede caps, and leather jackets, they seemed to be going to a wedding or something. "What's going on here?" I asked "Has there been a lynching, a plague? How come so many fled Poland to come here, show off your fancy wardrobe, take pictures at the Eiffel Tower and send them back as postcards to the old nest?"

They all smiled, pinching my cheeks. My village follows me from the very beginning.

Faivale Gutman here turns out to be a nephew of Lendov's marriage broker, Jaje. What a small world! I didn't remember what he looked like. After all, he left more than ten years ago. He's just passing through

Paris; he lives and works in Marseilles and talks more than his aunt, which is saying a lot.

But, as the Scriptures say, a brother who helps his brother is a fortified city. Faivele himself took me to the back of the synagogue where the congregation housed travelers en route to the golden land or to work in the Argentine colonies of Baron de Hirsch, (if they still exist). While we walk he tells me that I could stay for a couple of nights. Then, all of a sudden, he broke out in uproarious laughter.

"Seeing you in those rags you're wearing makes me think of a Sholem Aleichem story. Do you know the one about the peasant who comes to Paris and asks to see M. Rothschild?"

"Why the comparison? That's a lot of chutzpah! I'd never do that to you!"

"I know. I know. But listen to the story: Our little man insists on seeing Rothschild, telling the doorman that he will exchange the formula for immortality for a mere three hundred franks. He's so persistent that they finally let him appear before the big man himself.

"Nu? Nu?" says Rothschild.

"Listen, Mr. Rothschild," he says, "if you really want to live forever, you should come to my village."

"Really? And why is that, my good man?"

"Because, sir, I swear to you, since the village exists, not a single rich man has ever died there!"

The sanctuary was a beehive of activity. Every throat grunted feverishly and every arm was like an acrobat's. Even the walls seemed to converse with each other!

"Is it always like this around here?" I asked.

"Yeah, most of the time. But today even more than usual because tomorrow will be an incredible day!"

"The one who said that is Elias Grauer, the leader or organizer of our textile guild," whispered Faivele in my ear.

"Is it a religious holiday that I forgot?"

"It could be a holiday or a funeral, we'll see. A jury of twelve French citizens will pass judgment on one of our countrymen, know what I'm talking about?"

"No, who are you talking about?"

"Ever hear about the poet Samuel Schwartzbard in your neck of the woods?"

"Can't say I ever did."

"Come with us to the court house tomorrow and you'll have something to tell the children of your grandchildren. And may both gods, the French one and Abraham's, have mercy on this brave man who has suffered so deeply because of that Ukrainian bastard."

"Why did he suffer? Tell me everything."

"Is it possible that you've never heard of the monster Simon Pettlyura?"

"Well, of course I have. Who among us doesn't know about him. But what does that have to do with this Schwartzbard here in Paris?"

"You ignorant peasant. Back there in the shtetl you're not part of the real world, are you! Always buried in your miserable garrets with your Holy Books!"

"Nu, already, you don't have to get all worked up about it."

Grauer was really irritated and dismissed me with a gesture. However, the other fellows talked to him and then, looking me straight in the eye, he said: "Pay close attention, peasant. Our great poet Samuel Schwarzbard, originally from Besarabia, found out that the Ukrainian ran away from the Soviets and settled here. So, he tracked him all the way down just like a hunter would track down a deer. He spotted him. Followed him. And in 1926, right in the middle of the street, in front of everyone, he shot him and handed his weapon to the police."

"Oy yoy yoy! And how did the poet manage to find him in this enormous city?"

"Samuel had lived here in Paris since 1906 after escaping the pogroms in Russia."

"Gottenyu!"

"In those days he survived as a watchmaker, but around the time of the Great War, he joined the Foreign Legion and even earned the Croix de Guerre for his bravery in battle."

"Tell me, Elias, how come you know all this?"

Grauer stopped, walked to the end of the room, and came back with a bunch of newspapers. *The Paris Echo, Humanity, The Morning.* "All these papers have been carrying his biography for a year and a half now, ever since the trial started. We talk of little else around here because we're so many Poles, Ukrainians. . . . Anyway, want me to finish the story or not?"

"Yes, of course, please."

"O.K. then, listen. In 1917, Samuel went back to Russia, decorated and everything. As part of the Red Army Guards, he fought against that soulless Pettlyura and his Cossacks who exterminated our towns of Jitomir, Proskurof, Berdeitchef . . . among the fifty thousand sent to the next life were Samuel's parents and some fifteen relatives."

"So god punished him!"

"Well, if you believe in him, yes by means of Schwartzbard. . . ."

"And god allowed that to happen?"

"Don't go blaspheming, peasant. So, as I said, the bloodthirsty bastard came to hide here with his wife and daughter as if nothing had happened. But, he was a regular at all the bars and was soon spotted."

"Almighty Lord of the Universe! Just like in novels!"

"I'd say more like a play with an improvised ending. But these are no old wive's tales, because tomorrow, little peasant man whose head is in the clouds, from what I can see, tomorrow will be the verdict. . . ."

That night I couldn't close my eyes. I kept thinking about the amazing coincidence. If I had delayed but one more day in Lendov, in Warsaw, or on the long road, I would have been told this story, but would not have been able to attend such an important event in person. And I promised myself that I would write home and tell them everything, knowing full well they wouldn't believe a single word. . . . It's still night when they hand me a tie and a fancy jacket. On that very date I inaugurated my life as a city man, inside and out, as you'll soon see. . . .

Back home, my father's job was to slaughter geese and other animals after checking to certify that they were healthy and safe for feeding people. You know that by god's law we must not swallow blood, source of life. I can still see my father in his short coat cutting the animal's throat and veins face down so it would die quickly, without suffering. He was an expert slaughterer. Only very pious men of exemplary conduct were allowed, by religious authorities, to ritually slaughter beasts and birds. Imagine what an honor! And that is why my father, Rebbe David, is also the town's judge. He is the person who fixes any trouble that arises when Tobias steals a chicken or Motale wants to break his engagement to Java. . . . These were the big trials of my village! Momma always helped with her common sense: "Duved, I notice that if you go too close to the fire you get burned and if you stay too far you freeze, so, try to find the in between distance for this problem and only then say what you think." And father always made the right decision.

Is there any connection between that life and this solemn October 1927 assembly where our poet is the defendant? Miracles don't happen everyday, that's true, but I sure was lucky to be in Paris at the right time.

Very rarely did she pay any attention to all the community arbitration that her father presided over at home. In fact, all the shouting and insults bothered her. These intruders occupied the living room sofas, making it hard to get around the house for hours. Most of the time the arguments were over unfulfilled contracts, unjust settlements, a lie given under oath. Only in very extreme cases did they go to a

Gentile lawyer, and then only after the efforts of the "internal arbiter" had failed. She was always amazed that even though Max was such a bad business man—who took care of the business? his wife Rifka—he would judge rightfully over quarrels involving huge amounts of money. Blindly, the entire congregation trusted his moral solvency blindly!

That's why the living room in the Our Lady of Carmen building would turn into a court house. Dozens of litigants, rich and poor, millionaires and ruined men paraded by, year after year, and there was never any objection after sentences were passed.

One night there was an especially loud session. Two brothers, Leo and José Glickstein, were arguing over a joint account. It was very late when they left and Max tiptoed quietly to the bedroom: "I managed to convince José to pay Leo the half he had refused to pay before; it was really hard to figure out who was right."

"So? Nu? How did you arrive at a decision?"

"I'll tell you, Rivkala. When sleep was just about to overcome me, I remembered something that happened years ago. I went to ask them for help for Trumel. Remember Trumel? He needed a hernia operation and didn't have a cent to his name. Well, I went to their store. José didn't even bother to raise his eyes from what he was doing, but Leo bought me a cafecito around the corner and said: "Here's two hundred and fifty from both of us, but don't ever tell my brother how much I gave you." And that's how it was. So, tonight I thought: they both seem honest and each has his own truth . . . but I believe more the one who, with his whole heart and never even asking the name, helped a needy person."

I tell you, Doctor, I swear I've never met a person with such natural ethical judgement about the laws of coexistence. . . . ❖

We left at dawn, got off at Dauphine Place and walked a few meters toward the Palace of Justice. From the minute he walked in I was really impressed by Schwartzbard. Tranquil and steady eyes. Wide black mustache. Hair a bit lighter and straight and parted in the center like Charlie Chaplin's. A thinker's wide forehead. To my astonishment, his defender was—a French lawyer? Maître Henri Torres. Someone you should always keep in your memory.

The hall was packed. They tell me that on the first week, there were thirty false witnesses, Ukrainians of course, who still referred to Pettlyura as "Our Dear President." . . . Can you believe that? The chutzpah! That was why Torres subpoenaed over ninety Jews, originally from Poland and Ukraine, now scattered all around the globe, victims or their relatives, marked by the assassin's signature. They came willingly to show their scars, their castration, their mutilation. God forbid!

Twice the magistrates banged the main table demanding silence because the insults we hurled at Pettlyura kept interrupting the session. And it wasn't until the sun began to set, after an unforgettable day, that I realized, as in a silent movie, that they had set our poet free! Everyone cried but he. And so we were avenged of that beast—cursed be his name—for the eternity of centuries, Amen!

On the train, on the way back, exhausted and hoarse, my companions sang hymns in French, applauded and yelled "Hurray for Pres. Duverger and the 4th Republic." "We did justice again to Captain Dreyfus!" "Now Emile Zola is Henri Torres!" "Long live George Clemenceau!" "Vive la France! Land of human and citizen's rights!" I remembered, even though only a boy, that those names caused great agitation in Lendov.

We were a brotherhood. I too sang a proverb I had memorized in religious school slowly and stubbornly when I was eight years old and was only now making my own:

> *"Como pasa el torbellino,*
> *así desaparece el malvado pero*
> *el justo para siempre es arraigado.*
> *Amen.*

Just as the storm passes,
so the evil one disappears but
the truly just are rooted forever.
Amen."

Much later, the great poet Isaac Leibush Peretz, my countryman from a century ago, handed me a truer explanation:

¡El mundo no es taberna, ni bolsa ni march a la deriva!
¡Todo es medido y pesado!
Ni se evapora una lágrima ni una gota de sangre
Ni se apaga inútilmente la chispa de ojo alguno.
Las lágrmas se hacen río, los ríos se vuelven mares
los mares, un diluvio y las chispas un rayo
¡Oh no creas que no hay juez ni justicia!

The world is neither tavern nor shop, it is not driftwood either.
All has been measured and weighed
Neither a tear nor a drop of blood will ever evaporate
Never does the spark of a single eye go out in vain
Tears become rivers, rivers become oceans
The oceans create a deluge and sparks ignite the skies
Never ever believe there is no judge or justice!

Did she fully understand at the time what an honor it was in 1958 to vote in the first democratic elections after twelve years of military tyranny? In elementary school, dear Mr. Benollin, the teacher, and later in high school, others like him quivered while explaining how electing a government by means of free and secret ballots would work. The children, bored and apathetic, copied the outlines in different colored pencils. When will the bell ring? What difference could it possibly make if the big shots at the Miraflores Government House wore hats or caps, or went hatless altogether with their skulls burning in the sun?

The Jewish School at the foot of Mount Avila was their not altogether unassailable fortress. Under suspicion by the regime because of their previous partisan activities, they were under constant surveillance. And yet, knowing this, the teachers were still messengers of ethics and civics lessons, history and geography to these well-to-do-children with no political involvement, whom they looked upon as fellow attendees at a political rally. Sometimes they even managed to have an unexpected impact. Then they might raise their voice, even a fist, and declare that liberty would arrive soon! Suddenly, from one day to the next, the good professor would be taken away. In fact, in just one year, they changed history instructors twice!

Three weeks after elections, Fulgencio Batista fell in Cuba, and when the guerrilleros from the Sierra Madre took over, the air became unbreatheable at home. Max didn't stop his speech making, not even to eat.

"Rómulo Betancourt's triumph here in Venezuela is nothing less than god's justice."

"You mean to tell me the Messiah finally arrived, Father?"

"Better than that. What happened was fair and right. This man has been fighting Communism since before the dictator Gomez's death and is someone who will know how to handle them."

"What Communists are you talking about? Really, Dad, you're delirious and hysterical. You even see Communists in the soup! Is that why we can't even eat in peace? Soon you'll be seeing Soviet spies in our closets!"

"Your generation is a bunch of ignorant and useless fools. Pity what we spend for your education. Make fun if you want, but remember my words today. When your friend Fidel Castro comes to Caracas it's to rabble rouse the people against Rómulo! Those bearded servants of Moscow! I recognize them, my child, because I've known them for over thirty years. Mark my words and if I'm not here, knock on my grave and say: Father, it happened just as you said it would!"

She put her all of her money on the loser. She threw away her first vote on a gorgeous hunk of an admiral! Sublime visual delight: Wolfgang Larrazábal whose only platform was his looks. ❖

Worms eat the dead and worries eat the living. Long talks in the cafes and a limited amount of francs to pay the hotel of Vielle-du-Temple Street hastened my destiny in just seven days. I promised myself that I would return to Paris as a well-dressed man. I'd visit its museums, breathe in the parks, and watch the serene Seine. Now it was just a stop on a hurried journey and I had a decision to make: Uncle Solomon. Where was he from? Poland. Where does he live? In North America for over nine years now. Cousin Boris. Where was he born? Lendov. Where does he live? Havana, Cuba. Nu? Where should I go?

While I pondered, the Americans closed their doors. The unions were protesting that the Europeans took the few available jobs, leaving thousands of their members empty handed. Have you ever seen luck like mine? Of all the millions of compatriots that came to the Golden Land, just my luck! Only I, who nurtured this yearning as if it were the most precious rose bush in an arid winter, only I'm refused!

Paris no longer meant the crossroads. I was disgusted. The only easy problems to solve are those of others. But I must go forward. I could go to Marseilles with Faivele, and be a garbage collector in a fabric factory. But something tells me I should leave for Cuba. . . .

The day before the boat was scheduled to leave France, I headed for Le Havre on a train loaded with raw and cooked leftover food. After three hours, as the filthy train approached the coast, I felt a blue dizziness. Spasms and convulsions. The ocean was drowning me from afar. And when I jumped, as if I were falling into a liquid precipice, I thought: Oy vey, did I send cousin Boris the letter telling him of my arrival? I feared going close to the edge and being trapped by the waves. Neither the Vistula nor the Oder rivers or any other little Polish river could compare to this aggressive giant. Its salt burnt my eyes mercilessly. I confess I was petrified. For several hours I lie in the sand by the pier hoping my conscience would tame the waves. No, they will not swallow me anymore than they would those stevedores going in and out of the Niagara weighed down by their heavy loads. I had seen ships once before in a nonreligious book. I didn't understand then, and I don't now, how this gigantic barcarole could float. What held it up? Here indeed was god's echo. Blessed is he whose space has no beginning or end. Little by little, I accepted the fact that the horizon was a trick of the eye. Endlessness and god are one and the same . . . that relaxed me. . . . I could go confident because he would protect me. . . .

The bellowing seas of Saint-John Perse's poetry brought her to a new level of reading and away from the literature of ornate phrases, cosmography in symbols, and powerful sounds.

When she turned seven, they vacationed at the Miramar Hotel in Macuto, and at the first intersection of road and ocean, vertigo plunged her into total autism. Blind, deaf, and mute, it took a while to baptize her skin in that unique and violent immensity which until then had been paper scenery for imagination's travelers: witches, fairies, and magicians, the characters of Verne and Salgari novels, or Jonah or Simbad the Sailor or Robinson Crusoe.

How many oceans did she read about later until she arrived at Perse? Impossible to count. That rite of initiation repeated itself every time she came to the real sea, in the radiant burning on her eyelids, the saltiness on her tongue, a divine ecstasy where words become superfluous. . . .

By the time the ship reached the high seas, my stomach and head crashed. I was plunged into a profound abyss. Falling and falling without being able to stop the motion. The *Niagara* was a merchant and passenger ship, but on those first days I couldn't care less about what was on board. I remained in my ten-person third-class cabin. A foul-smelling hole, without any light, with bunk beds one above the other, straw mattresses, a dining room with long tables and a single latrine for more than one hundred people!

Even when the ocean was calm, I still was dizzy, restless, and disoriented, as if a spiritual storm were gathering very deep within my body.

One morning I opened the hatchway and suddenly the whirlpool disappeared. After that inauguration, I began to breathe the sea air with pleasure and never again in my life did I get seasick. On the contrary, I'm the kind of traveler who can cross the choppiest waters without any upset to my system. Practically a born sailor. . . .

Mandel Katz, a Lithuanian, helped me through the bad times with lemonade and some pieces of bread. We became shipmates. He was a very pleasant talker and was returning to Cuba for the second time in three years. He distracted my fear of the mystery of the sea by telling me about life on the island. He said it was the Switzerland of the Antilles, just as President Machado promised his people in 1925 that it would be. Katz assured me that in order to accomplish this state of well-being, the president even went so far as to eliminate the very names of all political parties.

"I myself, my friend, have seen the general on the street, walking around with no fear, giving a beggar a hundred dollar bill and saying very gallant words to a passing girl. Can you imagine? Out of his own pocket he took money to build a hospital and an aqueduct. What do you think of that? Over there all the Communists say he's a dictator. I, on the other hand, think he's a magnificent man. He never bothers us. You'll feel safer than in your own village. I give you the word of Mandel Katz!

Two weeks later we arrived in Cuba. Ah! La Havana! Her sky is low and the deepest of blues. Near the port, her sea turns darker. I'm dazzled by the intensity of the burning sun and the powerful winds that thunder along the beach, swaying palm trees as if they were uncombed long-haired ballerinas.

I see Berele waving his arms. Thank heavens! He got my letter! He looks so old with his dark skin! Could he really be the pale and long-pink-nosed little Boris who left his village five years ago? The very same person my uncle and aunt cried over and reclined barefoot for seven days in sign of mourning?

¡Maní-í! ¡Maní-í!
Si te quieres por el pico diver-tir
Comprate un cucurruchito de maní . . . Maníii!

Pea-nuts! Pea-nuts!
If you really want to have a lovely time
Come here and buy a hand-ful of pea-nuts . . . Pea-nuts!

This and other sensual sounds sweep me up from the minute I set foot on the ground. Men, women, and children selling lottery tickets, shoes, food, newspapers, anything you could want. Their hawking cries harmonized like a joyful chorus of prayers.

Listen, god, if you don't help me in Cuba I'll have to go begging to my uncle in America! What I was asking for was not peanuts because just then, and as if to prove my point, I broke out in a cold sweat as I heard someone yell: "Hey, Pole, pay your Tiscornia!"

"What does he want, Berele?"

"Wants to know if you have the thirty dollars to come into the country."

"Are you nuts? That's all the money in the world! Where am I supposed to get that kind of money?"

So, they detained me in Tiscornia, which was like Ellis Island and where I almost died of thirst because I refused to swallow the muddy water they gave me. Toward nighttime, my cousin came back with the money, borrowed from his girlfriend Rosa's relatives and other friends.

At last I could yell: "I got to America!" Maybe not the golden one to the north, where Uncle Salo had a steady job making suits in a workshop, but this equally golden place, la Habana. Even from the ship I smell the tantalizing perfumes of ripe fruit which this land gives off. You can become intoxicated without ever drinking a single drop of the "burning water" that the Cubans love. All you need is to inhale the aroma of melons and guanábanas and zapote and mangoes and coconuts and papayas and . . .

On the bus, Berele was talking and laughing but I couldn't pay any attention. I was amazed at the tall buildings, just like the ones they say are in New York, and big mansions, just like the ones in Warsaw, and the cathedrals, smaller than the ones in Paris, and along the beaches, incredible fortresses like the ones I saw in Germany.

"We're almost eight thousand workers in thirty branch brotherhoods all over the island."

"Then, Berele, can you please tell me what I'm doing here, a greenhorn, with no trade and not a word of Spanish? Am I just going to hang around with my arms folded? You know that the hardest job is doing nothing, don't you?"

"Take it easy. You just got here. Don't worry, there's room for you too. The Cubans like the Poles mostly because they're used to all kinds of people coming; that's how they came to be. The Chinese are called 'marras' and live altogether in their own neighborhood. The blacks work more in the interior, cutting cane ten hours a day on rich estates, shirtless, under the harshest of suns. They live, if you can call that living, in wood huts with palm leaf roofs. We make good money in the city. Don't worry and don't be defeated, cousin. Eat some of this roasted suckling pig and drink up your beer!"

At an inn, so full of thick oven smoke that I can barely see, I can recognize by smell, if not by name, what he was offering, and withdraw my plate in horror.

"Do you want some 'ropa vieja'?"

"I don't understand you, Berele."

"Why, do you need to eat something special?"

"Anything, Berl. Anything except pork!"

Fried plantain, sliced meat in a salsa, what do I know? I fall asleep on the bench, like a heavy war tank. It was so stuffy, I could hardly understand what Berele was saying. To make matters worse, he was speaking Spanish, forgetting that I was quite primitive, knowing only one language, that of our parents, a language, by the way, which he has almost completely forgotten.

"How about a cafecito, cousin?"

¡Ay Mamá Inés, ay Mamá Inés!
Todo lo negro tomamos café
Aquí están todo lo negro
Que venimos a rogá
Que nos conceda pelmiso
pa' danzá y bailá. . . .
Ay Mamá Inés, ay Mamá Inés!

All of us darkies drink coffee all day.
And here we are
We've come to beg
Please let us da-n-ce the da-ays a-way. . . .

The very first black man I ever saw was on the *Niagara,* and I'd be lying if I told you that I wasn't terrified until I realized it was not a monkey. That black fellow turned out to be better than several whites put together! The Cuban Liborio Martínez, fifty, maybe sixty years old? He was ageless. Let me tell you, the sun shines equally on darks and lights, but don't go imagining that Liborio was someone important on the ship. Nope. He was simply kitchen help, in the lowest class, which is, of course, where we all were. Like a good friend, Liborio always had a smile and a laugh.

So one afternoon, I said, "Hey Mandel Katz! I know you know a lot, but let's ask Liborio about Machado, O.K.?"

What's this strange fascination with blacks? Was it because a black man violated my mental innocence with playful treachery? Sadistic you might even call it, Doctor. Trusted employee at the store, Rafucho had an incredible voice and would sway his body to his Barloventan rhythms as he sang. That morning, left in charge of the five-year-old girl, he took off his pants howling with laughter. When her parents returned and heard about the performance, Rafucho disappeared forever. Forever? The rhythmic wail of spirituals, the tabernacle melodies of the Mississippi delta, was it mystical? voluptuous? classical? folk? pop? elitist? Does it matter? Trumpet solos, piano blues, and those voices propel her into lethargy while her senses are wide awake. Is there anything like jazz?

Later she fine-tuned. She added Martin Luther King and Louis Armstrong and Angela Davis and George Jackson and Ella Fitzgerald and Malcolm X, you and us, segregated minorities . . . aren't I doing a good job of analyzing myself, Doctor?

By the way, Doctor, you also seem to be mestizo, mulatto maybe? Am I hallucinating? ❖

Tired of my pestering, Mandel finally asked Liborio about Machado. And since, as they say, tongues have no bones, the black fellow let his loose.

"So you want to know about Gerardo the butcher?"

"His name is . . ."

"Listen, Pole, he and his father used to steal cattle in Las Villas, in my province. The thing is that when he made himself president, he burnt all the papers in the police stations so that nobody would remember. But it's known, Pole, it's known. . . ."

He spoke nervously, looking sideways to see if anyone could hear him.

"Machado, a butcher and thief? Are you sure of what you're saying, Liborio?

"Come closer, Pole. Yes! Later on he became very rich working with the gringos in the Electric Company, you see. But he still is the same butcher. For three years he's been killing and killing, only now it's people. They say he's up to two hundred ordered decapitated. Anyone who opposes him, Communists, students, workers, just anybody. Now hear me, don't you ever tell anyone that Liborio told you this, because, well, it might be bad for Emily and the kids."

Mandel turned pale, just like a cadaver. He wanted no more of Machado, and for the duration of the trip, he didn't even mention him. I also suspect that he didn't translate some things Liborio said so as not to scare me too much. But, so what? I would end up seeing this Gerardo for myself and pretty close up, while I collected glasses and cups on my first job as dishwasher in the Marina Bar where blacks weren't even allowed as servants.

One Sunday afternoon, the owner warned us about a special guest and the man himself arrived. Nu? What can I tell you? He was tall, good looking just like a movie star, though not as young as Rudolph Valentino whom we saw at the Niagara movie. A bit of grey, big stomach, and big protruding ears.

Observing all his details, I noticed that on his left hand he only had three fingers. Could my friend Liborio Martínez be right? Yanek the butcher, who's my father's helper in Lendov, also is missing fingers, and I'm almost certain it's from the left hand.

With his defective hand, the president grabbed the hand of an attractive woman in a yellow dress open all the way down to her waist. Together, with two military men, they drank and listened to danzones. It was twilight when the general got up and with a napkin tried to get rid of a spot on his shirt. A few minutes later, followed by a lackey carrying a little suitcase, he went to the bathroom, and when he came back, he was wearing a different shirt!

I didn't understand. It was difficult for me to follow. Hard to believe that this refined gentleman, upset because a single drop of liquid soiled his clothes, a man with such soft eyes behind his glasses, was the same who when nobody else was around they say killed four young workers, just the other day . . . in fact, one of was a landsman by the name of Noske Yalob.

"Listen, he put them in jail because they were Communists. He ordered that they be dropped, alive and tied, through a well at the fortress to be eaten by sharks."

We all trembled. Gottenyu, not even in the days of the tzar! Could this pervert be the same man whose picture I saw on the front page of the paper, with his very fine wife, when Coolidge, the American president came to visit a few weeks ago? Oy god in heaven, this was not to be believed. But you know, I guess I could see him . . . in a purple robe, pushing the dagger. . . .

I broke a few glasses and got insulting threats from the boss. I was being careless with my duties and the next set of broken things would be deducted from my pay!

Visions which seemed to be straight out of the Great War or the pogroms of the evil Ukrainians, left me no peace. I felt that all of Havana was a quiet terror because of all the blood being spilled by the *porristas* of the Patriotic Front, body and soul of the general. Dear gentle Liborio, are you well?

Special invitation. She was called to meet with them to demand: "Resign Rómulo!" and "New Government Now!" All the while, Fidel's firing squads execute anyone anywhere opposed to him. In and out of Cuba, everyone applauds. . . . Well, almost everyone. . . .

The meeting is at the Colinas de Santa Mónica, home of Humberto Rodanés where, so often in the past, they had all studied by the pool. Today, four professional waiters serve exquisite food to this select group.

"What's the big hurry anyway? Democracy was established less than a year ago and you're already advocating a popular insurrection? . . ."

"The interests of the people and the hopes of the masses are trampled on by the bourgeoisie with full support of Yankee imperialists."

"Listen, Humberto, I live in a very modest apartment, nothing like your parent's mansion here, and I put in seven hours of work a day teaching at a public high school. What do you do? Where do you work?"

"You mean you don't know? Right here in the party's young cell. But the purpose of this meeting is not to talk about our personal problems."

"Forgive me, but I'm leaving before you begin. I won't be going to the demonstration and I'd be grateful if you forgot my phone number altogether."

Cristina Doglio also left the meeting, but she didn't slam the door on the way out.

"Listen, Cristina, it's final. I have nothing in common anymore with those destructive maniacs."

"O.K. O.K., but why show them your anger? Do what I do. I pay as much attention to them as I do to the rain."

"Did you know that Humberto has fathered two kids by some barely adolescent girls? And he brags about it to everybody! When I asked him how he managed to support two households you know what he said: 'That's their problem.'"

"Typical."

"Yeah, real typical. Tell me, what kind of a revolutionary is this macho guy? He's incapable of having a mature relationship with any woman and to top it off, admits his paternal irresponsibility with ease and delight!"

"Sermons make them laugh. They're cocktail party socialists, remember?"

She understood a little better when General Strelnikov of the Red Guard explains it to Doctor Zhivago: "Private life in Russia is dead. History has killed it. Feelings, emotions, poetic subtleties, all that has become trivial." And the doctor's lucid answer: "I despise what you say, but I wouldn't kill you because of it." Ah, Boris Pasternak, one of many Russian authors never mentioned in the department that granted her a degree.

Fidel's death squads and a visceral dislike of rulers and bosses, some of whom claimed to be educators like her colleagues, people capable of sending children as rifle fodder to demonstrate against the system . . . brave leaders from the shadows, with hands in their pockets, trying to hide the innocent blood they love to collect. . . . These "trivialities" marked her first defeat. . . . ❖

For a five-cent bus ride I could circle around the beautiful capital several times. I know a Pole can never be a bus driver any more than a black man can be a waiter at the Yacht Club but, boy, what I wouldn't have given to drive one of these buses! By now I knew the city pretty well. I knew for instance that Monserrat was where the cheap-sex hotels were and that Maceo Park was where you could see the peasants arriving from the provinces, wearing guayabera shirts with machetes tied to their waists.

From the window of the bus Havana was a carousel of marble white columns. Often I would get off at one of the wide avenues and sit on one of the walls along Malecón Walk. There I enjoyed the ocean and the most beautiful sunsets any human being could ever hope to see in a lifetime.

Noches cubanas
que en rico tul
deja a las almas
plenas de luz . . .

Sweet Cuban nights
in your sheer web
Souls are captured and freed
to enjoy your magic light.

Right around the corner from where the buses parked on Teniente Street is where a countryman found me a rented room. Later on from the train window, I entertained myself counting the thousands of yellow balconies with iron grills. Or I slid through Jesús María Street to watch the thick-lipped, big-mouthed black women.

I'm telling you, to see Havana is to love her. Needless to say, those pleasures didn't minimize my problems. I earned very little in the Marina Bar, so I was very interested to hear that they were hiring bricklayers for the construction of the new capitol building. But you know, empty stomach, empty brain. That's me. Can I tell sand from lime? Forget it!

Instead, I become old Antonio's helper. A black man crippled by arthritis, he sold fruits and vegetables from door to door. I got off the cart, handed out the merchandise, and took care of the bills. I earned very little, but I had a ball stuffing myself with wonderful fruit like guayaba and frutabomba. Also, dealing with the customers forced me to practice my Spanish.

Ah, my beautiful Havana! From all my walking and bus and tram riding, I found out you were really two cities in one. That royal palace over there in Marimar is the house of a countess, one of Machado's many lady friends. And, over there's the Emerald Country Club, lusciously green, without a speck of dirt. But, just as those who are satisfied don't hear the cries of those who are hungry, these people had absolutely nothing to do with the ones on the other side of town, in the Llega y Pon area where the general's killers often went looking for prey. Same thing happened when they descended on Las Yaguas. But you'd never see them hunting down the enemy in the ritzy El Vedado neighborhood. Oh no. It's really true, you know what they say: God loves the poor but helps the rich!

I bought myself a new banjo because I had to leave my old one in Lendov, remember?

En el tronco de un árbol
una niña grabó su nombre hechida de placer
y el árbol, conmovido allá en su seno
a la niña, una flor dejó caer.
Yo soy el árbol conmovido y triste
Tú eres la niña que mi tronco hirió
yo guardo siempre tu querido nombre
y tu, ¿qué has hecho de mi pobre flor?

In the trunk of a tree
a young woman carved her name under passion's spell,
and the tree, so moved
dropped a flower in her bosom.
I am that sad and wounded tree
You the girl who pierced my trunk
I keep your dear name forever.
But you, what have you done to my little flower?

I sang with my horrible accent, and was so jealous of the creator of those lyrics and rhythms. It reminded me of Loña Sats and the actress Ida Kaminska, my Warsaw Esmeralda, both so far away and unreachable.

Loña was my imaginary girlfriend in Lendov. One day she left with her parents. I missed her for a long time. Before leaving for America I found out through town gossip that she is a mother of two in Detroit.

Anda pensamiento mío
díle que pienso en ella
aunque no piense en mí. . . .

Go my thoughts and please tell her
I think of her even though she thinks not of me. . . .

Nice song, also composed by someone else, yet when I sing it, I see Loña-Ida's face.

Yo sé que nunca besaré tu boca. . . .

I know I shall never kiss your lips. . . .

From their love songs you can tell that Cubans are very sentimental people. I always thought that people like that, who can improvise such beautiful ballads and tunes must really hate blood. Whenever I sing their ballads, even today, I want to fall in love, give and receive a caress, find love's company. . . . I looked but couldn't find . . .

But, what was I doing? I had to make it in America, that's what I came for, after all. Some of my countrymen were shopkeepers in San Germán, Baracoa, Sagua de Tanamo. Should I go there or should I go to Camagüey?

Rosita had relatives in Artemisa where, she told me, some countrymen earned good money in small factories. Seems they folded tobacco leaves to make cigarettes while someone sent by the bosses read them the news, or love stories, or action stories so they wouldn't talk or fall asleep. I said a grateful goodbye to Don Antonio and caught the train.

The sun was even hotter in Artemisa since it had no sea breezes. Walking on the dirt roads was like walking on red-hot coals. Oy, you can't imagine how it burnt the soles of your feet! Anyway, all I had to do was ask and I found work in a shoe repair shop which I went to because mine were falling apart.

Before I left Havana, I asked Berele about Rosa.

"Listen, cousin, syphilis is not cured with neosalvarsán and besides, the victim always goes blind. I don't want some woman burning me. I love Rosita, she comes from a good family, and I'm going to marry her."

"Boris, I know we must pray to god to protect us from a bad woman, but we've got to watch out for a good one ourselves. I'm sure Rosita is a very fine girl, but what I'm really asking you is: does that mean are you staying here forever?"

"Of course I am. A week after I arrived, for a dollar a day, with a spade in hand, I cleared weeds, I slept in tents, working on the train tracks that reached Bayamo. After that, during the harvest, I cut sugar cane in the fields with Haitians. Now I have a better job. You know something, I won't always live in a dilapidated rooming house with Serman and Luski. But the deed's done. Cuba is my country now. And the party has a great future and a lot of power here. Of course, things will improve for me when our comrades are in power. It won't be long now until we get rid of that shithead and Machadoism is drowned, my cousin."

I trembled when I heard him because I've always known that he who makes arrows often ends up being hurt by one of them.

New relatives appeared! Uncle Boris Udelman and Rosita, what nice people! It was a miracle they managed to get out of Cuba on the first wave, the first "worm shift" Castro let out. With their three children, they now live in Miami, constantly alert to what's going on in their beautiful Cuba. They arrived in Florida without a cent because the revolution took everything, from their socks to their house, which they built twenty years ago at great sacrifice, after saving every penny for years. Who could possibly imagine this quiet cousin and his charming wife in clandestine meetings against anyone?

"Don't you agree, Uncle Boris, that the Cuban people, those miserable ones who never had anything, are really better off now with education, health, and work?" she asks.

"Bite your tongue, cousin! You don't know what you're saying, my angel. It's hell over there and what you call betterment of the people is a lot of propaganda, my dear. We really do understand and know all the stuff that's going on. There is more hunger now than before. And, why do you suppose Fidel won't open the airports and the coast to free traffic? I'll tell you why: because if he does that, his beautiful island will be left empty. That's why!"

In Artemisa I learned very quickly how to sew the top part of the shoe. My fingers shed a lot of blood before I saved enough money to send to my beloved parents: "Dear family, I finally have a real job and now I eat Moors and Christians everyday. Ha! don't be frightened, that's what they call black beans and rice. And on Sundays, which is a day of rest here, I can feast on chicken and rice and even an occasional gallego-style soup. . . ."

I ate well, but gottenyu! the heat was like a blaze that never subsided. Even the blacks used to what they call canicular or dog days of summer, worked in thin or no shirts at all and sweated like waterfalls. And how did I feel? Here, anyone can go wherever they want and for as long as they please, can sleep, drink wine, eat hot spices, get medicine, money, and work. So?

Ah, but I had fallen in love with Havana and missed her ocean, my new-found friend and cure for most of my ills. So, I went back. This time, with a trade, I got a job at a bigger shoe factory. Good salary, and finally, far away from the funeral pyre of Artemisa. But then, Oy veis meir! a worse threat perturbed my calm, much worse even than the climate: Politics!

You know something? Since childhood my heart has always been on the left, and not only because god in his wisdom put that noble organ on that side of the body. No, because in Lendov we would escape from religious school and, carefully hidden in the hut of a barn, would read newspapers that travelers and coachmen would often leave. I remember very well that the *Moment* and *People's Daily* would inform us about the revolutionary movements fighting for social justice. I identified with the Socialist-Zionist Poale Zion party, but was not part of the group that later followed Communist orders. We had different ideas but were never boxing-ring rivals, never.

Simon Grossman also came to our meetings. He was a follower of the legendary Vladimir Jabotinsky, born in Russia. He was already part of the first legion of our people fighting against the Turks in Palestine and founded the first underground regiment of men and women to counterattack the Arab terrorists, over there in the Holy Land. Jabotinsky was such an anti-Bolshevik, he even joined Petlyura's brutal Ukrainian nationalists, the ones that used to go around burning our villages. I personally thought it was insane to make deals with the enemy, but . . .

Another one who used to come to our secret meetings was Erlich Mutnik from the Bund, the workers' antizionist and antireligious party. Can you picture so many differences among so few people? But that's how it was. I respect you; you respect me.

Well, we kept up the habit in Havana and a few of us would get together to chat. Very late at night, after the first and second floors and the yard were quiet, if nobody was hanging around the corridors, and after closing the curtains and doors, we would discuss the differences and similarities between socialists back home and here.

Shames, Migdal, and I didn't want to join the Communist group of Havana Poles because they were a cell of the Cuban Third International for over four years now. Grinberg, Semjovich, and Gurbaj, on the other hand, were like Yoska, Yunger, and Felix, club and union leaders who put out a weekly called *Justice*.

Others founded *The Communist,* also published every seven days, and both sides attacked us fiercely because we refused to be pressured into obeying Moscow. My bubbala Perl used to say that if you can't bite, don't show your teeth. But, we were naive and decided to publish a little sheet to defend ourselves. All this of course with the greatest care because if Machado's police ever found out about our activities, each of us would have ended up at the place from where no one returns.

So, we would attack with great cunning. Verses, satires, and prose which only the Reds understood but not the government, just in case a page should end up in their blood-stained hands. One January night, of the second and last year of my stay in Cuba, we went from one thing to another in a nightmarish meeting with Yunger and company, who were now leaders. You know how it is: Those who can't sing become song experts.

"O.K., you guys, are you joining the party or what?"

"Never. You're wasting your time pressuring us."

"Do you realize how you're hurting our cause? You're anarchists, that's what you are."

"I never have been, nor will I ever be a Trostkyite!"

"Me neither."

"Me least of all."

"Well, here you are anarchists because you isolate yourselves and you disobey our strike order."

"And that means anarchism?"

"Without a doubt. We don't smoke the same tobacco or drink the same rum."

"But we are true socialists!"

"Oh really, so what about your sheet and all the insults?"

"Well, you attack us in your newspapers, don't you? All we're doing is defending ourselves from your false accusations."

My father would always say that before saying a word think about whether it would still be good tomorrow. When our old companions' attitudes changed in tone, I stopped participating in that rude verbal tournament. Fights are like having fleas; the more you scratch the more it itches. On the other hand, it's wrong to insist too strongly on being right. If you threaten it's because you ran out of ideas. I thought of all of this while voices were being raised to a dangerous pitch.

So, at the next meeting of our group I asked: "Why did god give man two ears but only one mouth? So he should hear more and speak less. If you guys didn't learn this in your village schools, it's about time you recognized four kinds of people. Pay attention. The common person says what's mine is mine and what's yours is yours. The eccentric says what's mine is yours and what's yours is mine. The saintly one says what's mine is yours and what's yours is yours. And the wicked one, my friends, he says what's mine is mine and what's yours is also mine. Did you understand that? We are surrounded by evil people so it's prudent for us to remain silent. After the last meeting I realized that we have oil on our hats and therefore should not walk in the sun, if you know what I mean. The next time we meet with them, remember that a fool says what he knows, but a wise man knows what he says and what he should not."

Done. One unforgettable afternoon in April, we gathered in the House of Culture, with Semjovich and his disciples. I swear to you I was in great pain. My brothers were undertaking journeys that lead nowhere. Nu? I ask you? Who needs grey hair if their brains are green? As we expected they got upset because "not answering is an answer." Before leaving they spat out the final threat:

"We're leaving, little brothers. It's enough. We've lost our patience. It's bad enough with the enemy outside. Join us or you'll have to suffer the consequences because we will not allow our movement to die. You've been warned!"

When the bastards left and we got over the shock, I tried to present an argument: "When there are no alternatives, what's the good of being frozen in fear? I personally prefer life and liberty. . . . Let's escape friends. . . . Seems our only hope. When a man is drowning he'll even grab the tip of a sword in order to get out of the water."

I noticed that the mere mention of escape terrorized the group more and more. "Whoever is not willing should stay here and join them because if you're afraid of leaves, you shouldn't risk entering the forest."

"Don't you think we should ask for exit papers again?"

"You know that our elegant countryman Guggenheim, illustrious ambassador of the U.S. here in Cuba, never even tries to get us visas."

"What if we wait a little more?"

"Are you going to sit around and wait for our very own brothers to light the torches and turn us into ashes one by one? Abel sacrificed by the hammer or the sickle or both?"

"What if we ask Machado himself for the visas?"

"What? You know very well that his feared secretary Viriato Gutierrez sends anyone away who asks for a date at the Government Palace. Who the hell is a Pole to expect not to be turned away?"

"O.K. Suppose we decide to flee, how are we going to manage that?"

"Well, we'll have to think it out carefully. For the present, it's just a pact of silence because your ears are your own, but your tongue is heard by others. Second, don't harbor any illusions. They're serious, and the evil impulse of these fanatics is like a yeast cake. If you put it in the right place, it will always ferment."

The beautiful eloquence I laid out before my friends vanished by the time I got to my own room. What soap is to the body, that's what tears are for the soul. So, once I'm clean, I begin to weave the escape plan, always remembering that you must buy your friend because the enemy comes free. . . .

The university office is spotless. The tie and eyeglasses are solemn. "Licenciada, I've called you here to tell you that we cannot accept your application as a member of the department."

"But, you yourselves suggested and offered it to me when . . ."

"We don't have the budget for new positions and the one you applied for, by unanimous vote I might add, has been given to Rodolfo Alberto Sánchez Urdaneta who, as you well know, has been in exile."

"But . . ."

"Thank you for coming in. It has been a pleasure working with you. If there is anything we can do, please don't hesitate to stop by. Good afternoon."

She was blinded by shock and anger. Someone helped her to the ladies' room. Standing before the mirror she cried for a very long time. Enjoying the punishment? You poor little thing! Boy, did she feel sorry for herself. Sure. Good afternoon and good luck comrade Rodolfo Alberto. It's been done before and will be done again. Buyers of all kinds pursue her and tired, end by withdrawing their offers. . . .

Maybe because she hated business so much she doesn't know how to sell herself. Or maybe the price is too high. No doubt she is more expensive than activism. ❖

At the very time we were so tense over the preparations for our escape, I got a letter from Fashme, Lendov's watchguard. When we used to escape to talk about socialism, he was the one in charge of whistling an alarm if he thought some townsperson was getting too close to our hiding place. He feels lonely and far from us. He asks if he should leave for America.

"Oh, Fashme, my friend! Forgive my harshness but your question is idiotic. You're smart enough to decide your destiny without anyone's advice. Don't count other people's teeth. If you want to see the world, find the money for the trip, leave home, and walk under the stars between forests and rivers. Listen, since I left, I've gone from one corner of the world to another. I had hoped to start earning a good living soon, but actually, up until now, it's been pretty slow. I sold tropical fruits from door to door with a kind old man. Now I work at a shoe factory and things are going better. But let me tell you, everyone, whites, blacks, yellows, and even us, are liars. The journey to new lands throws you into a bazaar where everyone is trying to make a fool of everyone else. If you come, Fashme, you'll become part of that well-oiled wheel and will forget everything you ever learned at home. It's just a matter of getting used to it. Even so, don't think you'll find gold on the streets like manna in the desert. Sweat and more sweat you'll shed, let me tell you, before you see a few coins for your daily bread. That's if you're not betrayed first."

That's what I wrote, believe it or not.

Finally the pact of silence worked. My friends understood that everyone has to pretend not to know anything once in their life. There were six of us on the team, two Italians, one Armenian, and Daniel Alzu-Faray, the Cuban, who a few hours before our escape said, "I may end up covered in blood, Pole, but I'm going." A real mensch whose name I never forgot.

Until who knows when, my beautiful Havana, Cuba! I'll carry you in my prayers even though now, as I sneak around this embankment of the bay under cover of darkness, you no longer smell quite so sweet to me anymore. Now I smell a hidden stench, blood spilt out of sheer cruelty. It's a scent that makes you want to puke, a scent which no amount of sweet tropical breezes can overcome.

Good-bye Berele and sweet Rosita, Gutlib and Varnovski, Mitrani, Shlensinger, Rosencranz, Imiak, so many brothers and friends. What will become of you and, for that matter, of me? Last February during Carnaval, some of you sang Ochún, Babaluayé, Obatala, jumping to the rhythms of the bongoes. You even dressed up like Spanish ladies with castanets, black countesses, mulatto queens in cotton wigs, slaves and slave owners. You all swayed together in one feverish mass. Wonderful theater but I enjoy it from across the street, apart from all of you.

Remember when we all went to the town of Jacomino? Some of you even joined the procession of the Virgin of Santa Bárbara, walking behind her statue as if she were a living goddess. And again another time, I watched from a distance as you became part of the festivities of Saints Chango, Yemayá, inside that little hut where Toñito the baker took us. Dressed in white from head to toe, you crown a little girl as queen, cut off the white chicken's head, put on necklaces, and chant to Ochún, Chango, Ogún, Elegua until a man named Godfather almost baptized the lot of you, mesmerized and so full of lust!

And I? I was on the sidelines, wanting to leave as soon as possible, just like now, to run and jump into the motor boat waiting for us. . . .

If only they'd get a break! Just one month without having to write essays: Pesach, the Warsaw ghetto uprising, week of the tree, the miracle of the seven illuminated days at the time of the Maccabees, new year, Day of Atonement, the holiday of Esther. And how much longer with me in the role of prima donna? "What a beautiful voice!" they all said. But the repetition made it mechanical, not at all lyrical, just dull. . . .

The teen parties were her escape. Her body contorted to the rhythms of "Without You" of los Panchos, "Cinnamon Skin" by Bobby Capo, "Mambo" of Perez Prado, "Don't Ever Forget Me" by Rafa Galindo, and the "Guarachando Siempre Guarachando" by the Billo's Caracas Boys. It was a silly beat called "sabrosura." She tried to keep in step like a convulsing somnambulist, as if she were part of a ritual. Like being in society but not really a part of it.

She navigated through oceans of rhythms. But one, by Daniel Santos, really disturbed her:

Preso estoy
yo estoy cumpliendo mi condena . . .
La última, la única y primera para siempre
es la palabra
libertad.

I am a prisoner, serving my time . . .
the last, only and first forever
is the word
freedom.

The intimate and private moments were of course reserved for special idols: Beny Moré and Juan Arvizu and Alfonso Ortíz Tirado and Pedro Vargas and Frank Sinatra and Nat King Cole . . . such deep and moving cadences. The other had been a whirlpool without bottom, in which she gyrated in space holding on to the wind. Never really hers. . . .

Supposed to last four hours, our voyage becomes timeless. The little boat was rocked unmercifully by gigantic waves and blizzard-like storms as it drifted on and off course.

Without water or bread or shade, one faints from hunger, another hallucinates from thirst, and, on the third day, my townsman, Menachem Glantz, is driven insane by the sun. The ark lightens its weight as our impatience grows.

We were cheated. We had been promised that at a certain point and time, a trans-Atlantic ship, whose fixed route they knew, would rescue us as shipwrecks. It was the same trick used in other escapes and had never failed. Oy, gottenyu! How can you allow this when we've already suffered so much and we are so faithful to you?

"This mess is all your fault! You trusted Alzu and Alzu trusted that traitor and thief!"

"Please, friend, calm yourself, it's too late to cry."

"I'm jumping into the ocean like Glantz. It will be faster that way."

"Listen, even though Juancito is not a captain, he's a good navigator with a lot of fishing experience, and he's sure that the currents are taking us to Miami. Remember that the heart can always see more than the eye."

How slowly those torturous hours passed! In the quiet of the night, when no one watched, I licked my parched skin, drank my urine, and asked myself if our struggle to be free could possibly end right here in the stomach of a whale.

On the dawn of our fifth day, sparks flew out of the motor. Our helmsman, acting quickly, turned it off. He fixed it and said quietly: "One more night. I, Juan Ruiz, am telling you men. Hold on . . . don't give up!"

And so, when the moon rose, all were ready to sleep, assured that the end was in sight. The little boat would either be our crib or our coffin. No one cried anymore. No one argued. The scream of "land" woke us and we jumped like newborn goats. Juan, trembling, crosses himself. How short-lived was this happiness! While we looked at the coast, the bottom of the boat crashed against a pile of rocks! It was as if the curses of all my town's gossips had reached us at once, believe me! The bottom split just as we could see the beach in front of us! For a second we were stunned and paralyzed. But I reacted quickly, yelling:

"Don't think of anything, brothers, the shore is life! Let's jump. We've already lost four. Let's not give the sharks anymore of our flesh! There is a tomorrow, believe me! Everybody, swim!"

We jumped, and when we were a few meters from the shore, we noticed that Pesaj had stayed behind stunned by dizziness: "I can't, I have no strength," he whispered.

"Yes you do, just a little more, come on!"

"No, it's useless . . . I beg you . . . write home . . . tell them that I stepped on land . . . I beg you . . . say Kaddish seven days for me. . . ."

Juancito turned around and put him on his back, but it was too late. His spirit had already flown away.

On that unknown sand, half dead ourselves, we buried Pesaj Loifer. When we ended the prayer "may His great name be magnified and sanctified," we ran, naked and free of guilt, to swallow the green liquid of the puddles.

"No, my friends!" our guide interrupts. "That's the salty leftovers of the waves, and it makes you thirstier! See the little house over there? That means that there is sweet water nearby. Right here, spiders going into their caves! Hang on and let's lift the rock!"

"Sweet and blessed water!"

We drank like beasts during a dry summer. But, just as I told you, the evil eye was with us and suddenly, boots, boots, and more boots appeared.

"What country is this?" The rifles arrest us without answering.

From the smelly truck that takes us to jail, we can make out the profile of a modern city. Nobody asks anything anymore. All we want is water, food, and bed. By dawn of the next day we're informed that it will be a long lock-up because we entered the country illegally.

Did we hurt someone? Did we kill anyone? Did we break any locks and steal? So I wrote in a letter from the Tampa jail explaining our misfortune to the world. At the end of the ten weeks they'll send us back to Havana, and if Machado won't take us, we'll be sent back to our country of origin. In other words: the death sentence!

Alzu hands the envelope with my letter to a guard. An angel from heaven born in Cuba who had escaped almost the same way we did a few years back. He will become the anonymous hero of our adventure. Without batting an eye, he mailed the letter addressed to Uncle Salo in Brooklyn. Uncle Salo gave it to Baruch Charne Vladek, editor of the *Forward,* which had already published some of my poems written in Lendov and Havana.

This time I signed with the pen name Itze because I spoke on behalf of the whole group. I portrayed the truth about our imprisonment in the strongest possible words: that they treated us like animals, that we got no water, soap, towels, or sheets. What is the democracy of a country that mistreats the survivors of such a savage tyranny this way? That very day and without knowing it, I wrote a new birth certificate for all six of us. May god protect and keep you, guard without a name! He who gives as easily as you, gives twice!

You know of course that when brains are needed, muscles won't do. I drew our cell as a pit without air or light. "We are a group of fighters for a life of freedom. Is this a crime? Are we beasts, to be locked up because we flee certain death in Cuba? If they hold us in this 'democratic' cell only to send us back to the island, Machado will be able to save himself the trouble. Why? Because we will die long before deportation. Why? We will be buried soon because of a sickness that overcomes the malnourished: tuberculosis. The leftovers they hand us can starve even the strongest. The ones that survive will succumb to the terror of facing that depraved one who rules Cuba. Dear editors, I beg you, let the people hear this call for help. Our address is the State Penitentiary, 1503 Perice Street, Tampa, Florida. In the name of all those of us unjustly incarcerated because of our passion for liberty, Itze. May 14th, 1928."

Published on the 20th, we were out by the 24th with a two-week leave to look for a country that would take us.

My denouncement of our treatment in the paper, which appropriately is called "Forward," proved something amazing. It proved that the tongue is mightier than the sword, because by writing, you can wound deeply even from afar. . . .

All she really wanted was to write, but instead became a prisoner of senseless routines: Thesis in Tom. Advanced degree in Dick. Professorship in Harry. And, teaching everything, anywhere. . . .

To each his own. She had to get used to the fact that all she could do was give orders: demand to know where the direct object pronoun is; order the immediate count of the number of syllables in the verse; insist that all pronouns be identified so they don't disappear; command that all nouns be qualified, for under no circumstances should they be lonely; and require the identification of all metaphors in the following fragment of Arturo Uslar Pietri's works. . . .

Poor little ones! This emaciated one is from the very poor Pinto Salinas neighborhood. Several times already, my child, you've been suspended for seven days because you didn't wear the required uniform. What on earth will you be able to do, after these six years of primary education, with this arsenal of nonsense they throw your way and call grammar? Will you learn to write? To think? Or even to work if you can recognize the verbal or subject predicate of a sentence written thirty years ago by José Rafael Pocaterra? What if I lent you Memories of a Venezuelan in Decadence or Uslar Pietri's *The Red Swords,* so that you can read them unabridged instead of these school editions, could you discuss them? What ever happened to those great primary school teachers like Professor Benollin who always gave us mandatory written papers?

She writes to the chairman of the course. She writes to the chairman of the department. She writes to the chairman of the division. She writes to the superintendent of schools. She argues that this type of education will lead to mental retardation of several generations, not to mention national disaster. She writes encouraging them "strongly" to read the works of experts like the Polish teacher Janusz Korczak and the universally known Simón Rodríguez, teacher to none other than Simón Bolívar.

She became persona non grata. A stone in the road. A rotten apple. . . . And what about her letters? Could they still be in some ministerial office file or did they go directly to the waste basket?

The system lacks ears for this type of nervous disorder. You may not believe, dear Doctor, but that's how it is. . . . ❖

After a miracle happens, you can see it was not so supernatural after all. The short space of time that the American government gave us turned out to be a noose around our necks. Of course it's good to have faith. What's useless is to depend on it. If you just sit, thinking that you could become very intelligent, you'll end up an idiot. To tell you the truth, I no longer believed in America the Golden or its laws. But, I was alive and free. So, now I had to look for another land. If you break one leg, thank god you didn't break both, and if you break both, thank god that your head is whole.

Accompanied by Shames but lonely, I walked along the beaches of Tampa, thinking a lot. Yesterday is past, today is future, tomorrow is unknown. Who wants us? What nation on the globe needs two more Poles? You know, I often wonder whether hell is as sinister as the road that leads to it. Like pariahs from the Siberian steppes, we roam the shores of the millenarian ocean. . . .

"What's the matter, young men?"

I understood very little English, but there was a warmth in those deep green eyes, in that very pink face surrounded by very yellow hair attached to a very well-dressed man. White suit, white shoes, white hat.

"We don't speak English."

"Oh no? So what do you speak?"

"Polish and Cuban."

"Aha! I see. You're what we call *musiús*—foreigners—in my country. But, you speak Spanish pretty well."

In a gringo-Spanish, on the terrace of a fancy hotel, while we devoured sandwiches and sodas that he paid for, Mr. Warren Johnson told us his story.

"Why I was even younger than you fellows when I left this country. I worked in Guatemalan plantations. I traveled throughout Central America, by train, loading bananas, and ended up in Maracaibo just as they discovered oil. So, I stayed."

"Maracaibo?"

"Yeah, a lake full of it!"

"And where's that, Mister?"

"In Venezuela."

"In what part of the world?"

"Not far from here. South, about five days by boat. The doctor who takes care of the president of the country is a good friend of mine. A graduate of the Sorbonne, he took care of the president's urinary tract problems which had not been cured with the corn brews and other herbs he had been given. Under his care, the president, resurrected and grateful, gave my friend part of the Lake of Maracaibo."

"And can people give away lakes, Mister?"

"Over there they can."

"How's the climate?"

"Very nice. Warm and temperate. Temperatures are never too high or too low. As I was saying, my friend the doctor accepted the gift and sold it to the Caribbean company because . . ."

"There's work there, Mister?"

"Sure is. You could live in peace. Nobody bothers foreigners over there. In my adopted country there are no wars."

"How could we get the papers to go there?"

"No problem. I'm leaving in a couple of days. I'll take you with me and take care of all the paper work. I'm a Venezuelan and a friend of the president's savior. . . ."

The American government had given us a few dollars for one week's worth of expenses. On the night of that fateful day, in the cots of the only hotel we could afford, we think about and weigh Mr. Johnson's tempting offer of the sun and the moon.

I think out loud. "Travel always opens up the option of a new history and a crazy traveler has more choices than a sane man trapped at home. Don't you think so, Shames? Better a hen in the hand than eagles in the air. No? If you watch carefully you will notice that we poor serve god's designs because we make it possible for the rich to do good deeds."

Shames decided to stay. I left with the money that Mr. Johnson lent me to buy a ticket for the Louisiana on which he had a reservation. Of course I never saw him. I was in third class with part of the crew.

I knew that my rebirth was due to fate, and yet I was sad. Even to remember my state of mind then bothers me. I felt like a strange tree, with roots but without dirt or water. So you're alone, so big deal, what's the problem? If you carry your own internal light, you can illuminate any darkness, no matter how gloomy. I kept saying this to myself, but let me tell you, it wasn't easy.

When I saw the port of La Guaira I thought to myself that we must have landed at the very edge of a jungle. Nothing but a bunch of little houses, like the Cuban huts, only on a steep reddish hill. It was very clear to me then and there that I hadn't exactly landed in Manhattan. So what if you have to travel a five-hour treacherous road to get to Caracas? Would it have been any easier in Lendov? I have one mission here. To live.

In the very center of Jerusalem she found her own deepest center. How strange. That lugubrious hole of stone where the Holocaust palpitates on exhibit—Yad Vashem—is luminous, like a great sun in the midst of a long night.

Soaps made of the fat of your obese uncles. Locks made of gold teeth pulled out of the mouths of your sweet cousins. Lamp screens made of the soft skin of their little children. Can a museum show such concrete horror? They call it Yad Vashem, "never to be destroyed," said the prophet Isaiah.

The hands that carved this monument with aggressive piety in order to denounce the complicitous silence of the world are the very same hands that sow trees and roses at every step of the narrow sandy corridor, finally granted, their national home.

Israel was a profound certainty. Nothing could be further from living for living's sake. Nothing could be closer than living in order not to die.

Anyway, she was a tourist and vacation was ending. Return to the Diaspora.

When you move from one house to another, all you need is an extra shirt, but when you move from country to country your whole life changes.

The rich gentleman's house was in the elegant El Paraiso neighborhood in Caracas. I slept in one of the rooms in the back patio with the butler, a heavy-set, olive-skinned, middle-aged man who tells me that he was "born by the most plentiful of rivers, the Orinoco. I used to be a rural school teacher in Guárico, near Miss Beatriz's estate, you know, Mr. Warren's wife. Great land out there, and great hunger too. The only one who eats well is a Turk, Mr. Elias, a compatriot of yours."

"Yes, Mr. Luis José, I know for a fact that the poor suffer only twice a year, in summer and winter." The uproarious laughter seals a faithful friendship broken only by his sudden disappearance, but that happened much, much later and is another story.

Through a large window I could see the Johnson family living room. It looked like the only museum I had time to see in Paris. Crystal chandeliers, a sideboard full of porcelain figures, a flower vase shaped like a woman carrying a flame and suspended by golden angels, and a wall-to-wall mirror where everything glittered. I wondered what those little pink snails in each corner were for?

It was embarrassing to keep eating at someone else's table. Even though sleeping well is the best healer, on a borrowed bed my nights never end. During the days I walked around like a lost soul. Poor and with no news from home, how can I sing to the lord in this strange land?

Of course my unhappiness didn't stop me from taking long walks or from admiring the incredible transparency of this valley's light or its impressive Mount Avila. In fact, its monumental presence is what reminds me of where I am. Otherwise, Caracas actually reminded me a lot of home with its cobblestone streets full of little burros loaded down with furniture, bird sellers who line up their merchandise on the sidewalks, and coachmen delivering milk in big metal pails. Yeah, it actually reminded me a lot of my Lendov.

And yet, even though the grinder's whistle sounds just like it does back home, I have noticed that here work is divided according to people's national origins. For example, the black coffee carts and vegetable and flowers stands are run by Spaniards from the Canary Islands, the true virtuosi of all street vendors. All day long, as if you were at an open air opera, you can hear their voices: "Island Bread!" "Hot arepa breads, three for a nickel!" "Carnations and lilies!" "Coal a quarter a kilo!" "Daisies!" Just like in Havana, their songs become a background chorus to the church bells which ring every hour on the hour and can be heard throughout the city. Italians, I've only seen two. One, wearing brown flannel pants, was playing a little organ by turning the handle while kids yelled "piano musiú!" I was enraged because they were making fun of him as if he were a clown. The other—oy gottenyu, I felt such pity for him—in his filthy clothes and tobacco-stained lips, was gathering waste at the stockyards sighing: "Madonna mia!" "Madonna mia!"

I love the red and blue electric trains. For twenty-five cents they go from Puente Hierro all the way to Sabana Grande. I notice that some streets have high sidewalks with side rails and stairs at each end. Houses of one and sometimes two stories with beautiful grille work on their windows are lined up in rows.

Homesick and lonely I go out trying to find other Jews because I need to speak in confidence. In moments like these, the best prayer is an open heart. But no friends appear. Nu? I think. Isn't that the way it always is? When we laugh, everyone sees us, but when we cry, nobody does. I'm young, that's true. But only in their youth do trees bend, when a strong wind wants to test their fragility.

How much longer can I impose on the Mister and his family? I know that guests, like fish, begin to smell after the third day. So if for the first meal they served me chicken, and for the second eggs, why wait until they serve me leftovers?

Trying to walk off my *tzures* I get to Plaza España and cross toward the firehouse, where I see a beautifully planted garden near the building. By the fountain I rest at a bench, inhaling the wonderful fragrance of those exotic flowers.

Nearby, a short bald man is taking pictures with a four-legged camera, you know, the kind that has a little black curtain. It's been three years since I left home, and it would be nice to show them what I look like. Anyway, I'm not even sure they got the picture I sent from

Artemisa, of me eating lunch with all my co-workers at the shoe factory: the Polish women and their children, one or two white Cubans, and several shirtless blacks. (I chose to send that one home because I looked a little heavier and had a happy smile.)

I count my fortune in bolívares. Maybe I have enough to take a new picture to send with the next letter after all, none of my people even know I left Cuba.

"Sir, would you be so kind?" I try to make myself understood by showing him the little money I have folded up in my yarmulke (forgive me, dear god!) and suddenly, the photographer starts wailing in Yiddish: "Oy, oy, gottenyu! You're one of us! You're one of us." Samuel Vilner, who will be my friend to the very end, grabs my old and wrinkled yarmulke, kisses it, and cries: "Let's speak Yiddish,—*la lengua que se habla por si misma*—since it is the language of our souls. . . ."

That same afternoon I say good-bye to Mr. Johnson, promising him that I will return very soon to pay him back for all his kindness. I hug Luis José and with Vilner at my side, enter the rooming house where several other countrymen live. It is a fresh, clean house, with three patios, like parks, covered with plants and little flowers. It's between Guanábano and Amadores streets, near the Bridge of the Suicides (god forbid!), and on the way to the cemetery, called God's Children (may we never need it!). Despite all these sad names, the rooming house is full of life, or maybe I just think so because at last I've found the company I was so desperately longing for.

As soon as I walk into the dining room for dinner, my friends, without even letting me breathe, force me to repeat sounds like: *gracias* (thank you), *barato* (cheap), *cliente* (client), *marchante* (patron), *cuota* (on installment), *Dios se lo pague* (may God repay you), *misia* (ma'am), *ganga* (bargain). I feel like a kid, learning his first Hebrew letters in school. It's because I have to know the language of my new occupation, they all say, the language which will make me into a man with a steady job and a guaranteed income. King Solomon said that there is a time for everything in this life, so, every time of a person's life has its own language.

The instrument of imperialist intrusion. The language of capitalism. Phrases that had alienated her from the English language. And now—how embarrassing!—she feels her awareness of the universe limited because she neither reads nor writes that language. She had loved Elvis Presley and Jimmy Dean instinctively.

It's been a ha-ard day's night
and I've been working like a do-og. . . .

Sounds prosaic in Spanish, but when sung by four disheveled, long-haired kids from Liverpool with great sweetness it was absolutely liberating! What does this have to do with her? Nothing. And yet, the protest, shrouded in the sensual sounds of an electric guitar and their own beautiful voices . . . do they really only speak for themselves?

"Help! I need somebody's help!/ Not just anybody's help . . ." is the cry of all who are fed up with worldwide politicking. Are these guys businessmen? Are they hippies? Maybe. But a song like Once in a Lifetime is a hymn about urban ennui. It reflects the anguish of people all over the world, and, in a way, begs for the dissolution of useless barriers between nations.

That choral poetry was a shared experience, a poetry heard outside libraries where the bookworms gathered. The best sound in decades.

Yes-ter-day, all my troubles seemed so far a-way
Now they seem as though they're here to stay
Oh I believe in yesterday.
Suddenly I'm not half the man I used to be
There's a shadow hanging over me
Oh yesterday came sud-den-ly. . . .

Now sung by new troubadors, that beautiful language managed to say so much in so few words. And so, from Bob Dylan to Walt Whitman through Simon and Garfunkel, Joan Baez, Leonard Cohen all the way to Allen Ginsberg. . . . One less prejudice thanks to these contemporary minstrels, the great Beatles. She was about twenty-five years old (not exactly a teenager!) when all this happened. ❖

He who thinks he can live without others is very much mistaken, but he who thinks others can't live without him is even more mistaken. So, I got to do it, alone, with the package on my shoulder, and a pad and pencil. A city worker, finally on my own.

Without further doubts, I get on the Black Panther—don't be frightened—that's what we used to call the bus that went all the way to Laguna de Catia. I wander and wander just like a gypsy all around the blue-green lake but with no time to enjoy the tall bamboo, willows, and other shrubs surrounding that flat hole. Of course, a person can forget everything except when it's time to eat. Right?

Anyway, I go from door to door. By late afternoon my feet feel like pancakes, they're so swollen, and my back is breaking. But, I conclude that if a person looks for easy work, he'll go to bed even more tired than when he woke up!

While I waited for the return bus back, I prayed: "Gottenyu, please help me get up, I already know how to fall! I know, my sweet god, that miracles do happen, although yours rarely take the form of food trays! Anyway, please don't forsake me and I won't let myself fall. . . ."

That very first day I learn that the only thing that's free in life is garbage. I didn't sell a penny and returned before four. "Listen, people here are very nice. They never say 'No' to your face. They always say tomorrow, tomorrow," my friends say.

"Well, I sure hope so, because I'm going back tomorrow!"

My third Saturday on the job I walked from La Vega all the way to the hills of Petare. Then I decided to take a break and walk around the streets of Caracas with my friend, Nujem Vaisber. While conversing about our lives as door-to-door salesmen on the installment plan, I tell him that Mr. Warren never told me anything about the dictator, nor about how much he is feared by all. Without realizing it, we had entered the long narrow alleys of El Silencio neighborhood, near the Plaza Bermúdez, where one can see cheap-looking women and men, all made up, wearing earrings and bracelets. I was so shocked by this spectacle that I asked Nujem in Yiddish: "Does Gómez allow this?" Suddenly someone slapped us on the back: a man in a chocolate-colored uniform, straw hat, and *alpargatas*—black cloth shoes. He drags us, tied up like beasts, all the way to the San Juan parish police station, a few meters from where I had the misfortune of asking that question. From there we were transferred to police headquarters, about a half a block from the San Francisco church, which has a beautiful silk-cotton tree, right in front, and which is right in back of the capitol.

No one explains why we've been arrested. Who dares ask? We pass a corridor packed with soldiers holding their loaded rifles, ready to shoot even though they're seated on these long benches. We're pushed into the Flag Room, where an official is taking a statement from the agent who brought us in. We protest when we hear his accusations, but their ears are made of cement. Anyway, with all those soldiers ready to shoot we decide it's better to shut up. Finally they lock us up in a little room with a tin roof from where we could easily hear all the swearing and cursing of the drunks piled into the next barrack.

It was seven o'clock Sunday morning when they finally opened the cell: "O.K. Frenchies, grab your stuff!" Vilner and Davidovich and I don't remember who else, oh yes, someone named Mashlack, were our bailsmen and translated what I, in my Cuban-Spanish from Lendov, was trying to say. "Speaking of one thing and another, we were walking along, when I asked something about Gómez because

I've just arrived in Venezuela, and there is much I wish to learn. . . ." They send for the policeman who detained us, and when he appears an hour later, he points to us in a rage: "You should leave these in the slammer because they were saying horrible things about the general. Yes, sir. I heard it with my own ears. They said, 'Gómez.' Now they're pretending to be foreigners. Sure!"

So that was it! Did I ever mention the name Juan Vicente Gómez on the street again? Now that was a tyranny like no other, except maybe the Russian one.

In solidarity, the student organization decided to visit ex-guerilla Commander Alcides, Humberto Rodanés, in Caracas's New Model Jail. The visitors room is in the old slave quarters and so dark that they have to have a light bulb on even in the middle of the day. A gloomy spot that made a person wonder about the squalor of the rest of the place. They haven't seen him for seven years and are amazed to see his wrinkled face and premature grey hair. During the uprisings in Carúpano and Puerto Cabello, like a good bourgeois, she would always look for his picture in the papers, since he was a co-leader of the uprising together with the rebellious military. But it never appeared. Later they heard about his march on the state of Falcón to reactivate some of legendary Che Guevara's ideas. . . .

"Humberto, why did you guys insist on going on even after you saw that the people were not with you?"

"We were too idealistic, we thought ourselves Messiahs were going to awaken the people with their own heroic example of courage and sacrifice."

"Because of Sartre's exemplary 'action of the left' philosophy?"

"Yeah, it must have been that. We dressed in olive green uniforms, Cuban style, hoping to gain sympathizers for our cause."

"But even the union workers didn't pay any attention to you."

"Because the unions had been infiltrated by the government, that's why."

"And now, how do you feel now?"

"Physically fine, I've already gained a little weight. Morally, fucked! The problem was that we simplified the fighting plans. We copied Castro's charts without paying attention to local conditions. We were dogmatic and, like all mules, saw only what was in front of our noses."

They were all deeply affected to see a member of their own generation turned into an old man, "He matured the hard way, by suffering. What a paradox! In prison he became a free man!" they agreed. ❖

Our daily bread becomes harder and harder to get. Gottenyu is so just! He gives the rich man food and the poor man appetite! I keep body and soul together thanks to something called *majarete,* a pudding made of milk, sugar, and corn which you can get for a few cents at any corner.

One morning Moishe Goldberg, the stocking salesman, wakes up sick so he lends me his trunk. I hit the road yelling: "Mediahombre Mediamujer!" just as they had taught me to.

The passersby smile and some even break out in loud laughter. That night, Moishe, still weak, wets his pants from laughing so much when I tell him what happened. He finally manages to tell me what's so funny: the word *media* means both socks and half! So I'd been running around yelling: "Half man! Half woman!" "Half man! Half woman!" Yeah, very funny!

Another day I come home without a single sale. Furious, almost flying, I cross the three patios until I reach our room to yell at my companions: "Why do you guys lie to me with this so-called help? You give me clothes to sell and I can't sell them because the customers keep asking for something called *otrodía* and you guys never gave me that merchandise. Where do I get this 'otrodía' stuff? And remember, friends, half a truth is a whole lie!"

Convulsing with laughter they try to defend themselves: "Otro día" is "another day." You spent two years in Cuba working with natives and you still don't understand when the people here speak to you! Is it our fault you left your brains in Lendov? Your problem is that you keep thinking in Yiddish and that's why you can't get Spanish into your head. Listen, if you don't want to ripen you'll be green forever!"

Energized by an anger that grows with my benefactors' teasing, I compose a tune in our mother tongue and accompany myself with my third banjo. (As you probably guessed, it was impossible to bring my Cuban one with me.) I sing:

Todo el día, como de costumbre
hay que correr con el paquetico al hombro
y la mujer no te oye
no te ve
no quiere comprar.
Y si ya compra un trozo de tela
me escribe en la tarjeta
venga a cobrar el domingo.
Toco en la puerta de la vecina
y un niño me da la noticia:
la señora Petra se mudó
y vete ahora a buscar su dirección.

All day, everyday
we schlepp merchandise on our shoulders.
The woman doesn't hear you
doesn't see you
doesn't want to buy.
If she does buy a piece of cloth
she says: come collect on Sunday
I knock on the neighbor's door

and a child gives me the news:
Mrs. Petra moved away.
Now go try to find her new address.

When I end my song, smiles have disappeared from my brothers' faces. They're all crying like little babies. And upon request, I will cry out these verses again and again.

Let me tell you that despite my funny poem I know these people are noble. Most of the time they don't even need those rags we try to sell. But when they see you carrying those heavy bundles on your back, they feel sorry for you and buy something and pay one bolívar a week. They who themselves are barefooted buy from you on credit. When they don't even have that, they open their doors: "Come in musiú. Sit down a minute in the patio. These ferns provide a delicious coolness, come, have a cafecito."

I know the city by heart, the eighteen months of walking and walking are too much for my feet and not enough for my pockets. I'm a good-for-nothing. I can't sell anything. Could it be that I'm a born defeatist? If I sell umbrellas it doesn't rain. If I sell candles the sun never sets. If I sell coffins, people stop dying, and when I wind the clock it stops. . . .

What I earn doesn't even cover the expense of the license I need. They're asking ten thousand bolívares for it. And while taxes keep coming like rain, my sales are barely enough to survive on. It doesn't do me any good to make things cheaper than lettuce soup. I'm just no good at this.

"Go to Valencia. There you can collect and you don't have to pay government taxes."

"Really? And why's that, Goldschmidt?"

"Because it's the interior and all they want is thirty bolívares and you don't need to be sponsored by a merchant."

"Is that so? Well, I'm off then."

Before packing and moving to this so-called Valencia, I have a long talk with the Almighty and pray: "To you, god, I say this again. I know you're exhausted from all your work here on earth. I don't ask to be picked up, it isn't that. But, could you at least stop me from falling down so much? O.K?"

Valencia la novia del sol
su lago de límpido azul. . . .

Valencia bride of the sun
with her clear blue lake. . . .

She's getting married and the completeness she felt was love. Total sharing. They wanted a quiet wedding, nothing fancy. With the money set aside for the banquet, they bought furniture, and what had been saved for the wedding gown went to pay for a honeymoon to the Andes Mountains. Breathtakingly beautiful! And then, at the height of a horrible heat wave, they arrived and settled in Valencia for the next stage of their lives in a two-story house, on Páez Street. A Jordanian Muslim and his wife lived on the ground floor and raised goats and cocks.

Valencia es
cantar y florecer
ben-di-ga Dios
el valenciano amor

Valencia, songs and flowers
God will always bless
Valencian lovers. . . .

The stench that came in from the patio was a constant reminder that they were in the country now and had better get used to it. No matter what the circumstances, two professional graduates of the nation's public university had to repay the material and spiritual debt of their education with vigorous and free labor.

And so they arrived on a pioneering mission. Don Quixote and his Sancho Panza. The grieving nation awaited them impatiently. . . . To work! ❖

Through coconut trees, the narrow road crosses cultivated fields and underbrush near Maracay. Two hours later I get off at the last bus stop, the ARC right in front of the English Railway Station.

I walk a few meters on Colombia Street and I ask a pale "chicha" vendor for an address: "Hey Turk," he answers, "It's right there, around the corner."

It's five in the afternoon when I get to the Plaza Bolívar where all the benches are occupied by my countrymen. I recognize them right away. While I shake hands I give each my full name and where I come from. Then and there I make another life-long friend, Benjamín Landka.

They describe Valencia with great praise. And without meaning to, I remember the story about Chelm, the town of fools, where one day everyone decided to wear glasses that enlarge things. That way they said, things not only seem big, they really become big. Nu? Of course, Chelm was a monumental city! But, what am I saying? Don't pay any attention to me! That's nothing even remotely like Valencia. Soon I discover that, and I'm not exaggerating, it's a wonderful place to live quietly and work productively.

They all speak at the same time. They hug me and drag me to a big room with four windows where you can read on the door: "Room for rent to quiet gentleman. No meals."

"You know something, Benjamín? That sign fits me with amazing accuracy: orderly and starving!"

My future landlady is Micaela Huerta, an old lady with a long neck trapped inside a black blouse. She looks me over from head to toe:

"Are you a musiú?"

"Here, yes, Ma'am."

"Miss to you, if you don't mind. So, another junk-selling musiú."

"I think so, Miss."

"That'll be three a week, in advance."

At first I liked it. What's not to like? It had a beautiful garden full of small palms and dozens of pots full of violets and other flowers. And yet, seven days later I moved. Why? Stronger than the beauty and aroma of flowers was the stench of incense which, since childhood and whenever I passed the open doors of a church, would scare me to death. I never did find out where it came from or why.

So, I found a temporary room in Mr. Timenski and Mrs. Fefer's inn on Libertad Street. The food was good, but the bed! Oy yoy yoy! I'd rather not even tell you about it because it makes me itch all over.

Valencia, even more than Caracas, reminded me of Lendov. Its country atmosphere and slow rhythm made the seventy? eighty? countrymen become very close. All these men knock on doors to make a living. And Marta Fefe's menu is the final touch to get rid of or increase nostalgia. Chicken soup with barley, beet juice with potatoes, cherry pie with raisins, all the while she is complaining about the lack of an oven, the coal stove that makes her nose itch, and her skin rashes.

Later on, three of us moved to Mrs. Elodia Santana's house because with more bathrooms we avoided fleas and bad odors. You know, a salesman who sweats among towels, tablecloths, fabric, insects, and road dust has got to be a water lover.

A few days after we moved, Abraham Loines, a very religious guy from a small town in Besarabia, arrived. He began "making America" by selling ice cream in a little moving car. He shared the living room which had windows facing the street. Well, here comes the story.

Because of the intense heat, Loines would open the shutters when he got up, and after washing his body he would begin his morning prayer: "I thank Thee, living and present King, for returning my soul," and of course he had on his phylacteries, a little square box on the forehead containing four sacred passages in very fine parchment and the other tied seven times from the elbow to the wrist. While he prayed, Abraham *shokeled*, he balanced himself strongly forward, back, and sideways, in a true mystical rapture. So, every morning the neighbors would gather to see the *loco* with the black ribbons, as they called him.

I'm sure you can imagine how enormous the crowd was by the third day. Anyway, commanded by Doña Elodia, we went to tell Loines to close the windows. The poor fellow, a very strict observant of Divine Law, suffered a great deal over that. He said that in Hotin, his village, the Christians would always look upon these practices as normal and never paid any attention to them.

Eventually I was able to pay a young Gentile boy to assist me with my heavy sacks of merchandise. We did the town. Sometimes by trolley car which cost a few cents, but mostly on foot. We would leave from the 5th of July Street, go all the way to El Palotal, La Pastora, and El Morro. We left nothing out.

If only you could have seen me! I always wear white linen pants and jacket, a tie, a straw hat to protect myself from the sun, and tied leather shoes. I never wear the local slippers called *alpargatas*. Sometimes on Sundays, I wear a *liquiliqui*, a local outfit, high neck, no tie, also made of linen.

Our daily gatherings are still in the Plaza Bolívar. I often remember the time the very respected Mrs. Clara Landka, just arrived from Lithuania, felt very thirsty. Benjamín goes with her to find a drink. They get to the nearby corner bar on Faisán Street and the argument begins. He doesn't want her to go in because only sinners who drink and play pool and cards go into that kind of a place. Of course, she's petrified of staying alone on the street while he goes in. Anyway, King

Solomon must have illuminated Clara, because she drank her soft drink standing in the doorway, neither in nor out. All upset they return to the plaza, and Clara laughs so much that her husband has to go back to get her another drink so she won't pass out laughing.

Ay ay ay! Those were the days! One day we're told that Vilner came to try his luck in Valencia. When we finally found him, he was fast asleep in Doña Rosa Virginia's inn. We wake him up, he's glad to see us, jumps out of bed, and talks and talks. We talk as we walk down the street to our corner of the park where there is an open air concert. An orchestra plays beautiful local waltzes because it's July 24th, Simon Bolívar's birthday. When we get there we realize our Samuel is in his pajamas! Well, our laughter is so noisy that policemen and passersby approach us cautiously thinking we're escaped maniacs.

Little by little, the city, the people allow me the peace of mind, the serenity to write long letters to Lendov. I describe Valencia as a big town where I found something like a family. Since the population is not large, and the space is small, we all feel at home. We know we can reach each other easily in times of need or happiness.

I remember just one bad moment. It was the Sunday my friends went to the beach at El Palito and I spent the day collecting because I had to make up the time I had lost in Caracas.

I knock on the Rodriguez's door on Martín Tovar Street. "Come in, peddler."

"Thank you, Ma'am."

"You here to collect?"

"You told me to come on Sunday, Ma'am."

"Yeah, yeah, but first have a cafecito, it's early."

"Thank you, I really like the coffee here."

"Listen, don't you go to Mass on Sundays?"

"Mass?"

"Mass. To the church of our Lord Jesus Christ, you know?"

"Jesus you say?"

"Yeah, who else? Christ, you know, Our God?"

"Oh no, Miss Rodriguez, I don't pray to Jesus."

"You don't? And why not may I ask?"

You can't imagine how she changed. She turned pale. She jumped on the chair. Her eyes bulging. She didn't blink. Retreating without taking her eyes off of me for a second, she yells: "Begone Saturday!"

"No Ma'am, today is Sunday."

"You pray to Satan then, king of Saturdays, right?"

"What are you saying, Ma'am?"

"Holy Trinity! May God protect and favor us! That's why you work on Sundays! I just realized it!"

Desperate she began to call for her husband: "Gregorio, come quickly! Pay the Turk, once and for all. Pay him the whole two bolívares and make him never ever come back here again! Never!"

"But Ma'am, I brought the new curtains you ordered, they just arrived three days ago."

"I don't want your merchandise, not even if it were free. My God. I want the devil very far away from here! Santa María Llena eres de gracia . . . Hail Mary full of grace, the Lord is with you. . . .

At dusk when we all walk between the lush trees in Camoruco, I tell them what happened and Landka gets nervous. "Don't try to fill a sack full of holes. When you go into a customer's house, drink his coffee, but talk as little as possible about yourself. Only talk of sales and payments. Avoid all intimacy and that way you'll have no problems. Oh yes, and never stop by the windows to collect from the servant girls; that discredits the young ladies of the house!"

There was another memorable Sunday when we had to run like rabbits, all the way from the plaza, and take refuge in the Mundial Movie Theater. We had been laughing so loud that the guests at the Hotel Germany had complained about the noise. That same night we agreed to collect a few bolívares and set up our own club. Up until then, religious and family events were celebrated in the homes of the married ones, often at Haim Sunshain, a learned man, very knowledgeable about our history, and owner of the tailor shop. Because of his almost diplomatic wisdom, we all thought of him as our leader. Anyway, we never did rent a place because we were afraid of Gómez's police.

With our first collection we bought the Five Books of Moses, our liberator from slavery in Egypt. We ordered them from Poland together with a ram's horn for blowing on Yom Kippur.

The day that Landka came back from the piers of Puerto Cabello with the Bible in his arms, we celebrated with great emotion, and I, hidden in the Sunshain's bathroom, cried for Poppa and Momma, feeling it was high time to start a family of my own. But how? I didn't even look for hourly pleasure in the bordellos of El Morro because there was a syphilis epidemic just like in Cuba and all women, especially the streetwalkers, were contagious.

Should I bring a Jewish woman from Europe? Many of the men did. They met through letters and pictures. Their long-distance fiancées arrived here in Valencia alone or with relatives. Faier, the *moil*, like my Poppa in Lendov—may he have found peace—married them. A couple of times they didn't marry a second time in civil court, and as the kids got older they ended up marrying what the law calls their concubines. Otherwise, the children would have been bastards, without the father's legal protection or name.

One thing I'll tell you, each and everyone of them got married. Some sooner, some later. But they did. It's not right, god knows, to bring children into the world without the father's blessing and name.

We always took care to resolve all our disputes. For instance, if one of ours disappeared overnight with some woman or was playing cards somewhere in El Morro, as soon as the wife came crying to our door, we would gather a small group and go in search of the lost one. The one who really gave us problems was Jacobo Zerate. Stubborn and greedy, big mouthed and small hearted. He refused to bring his wife and two children left behind in Galitzia. We scolded him day and night. Then finally, the miser spent his money and brought them from Poland. No wonder they say that when you shake hands with a Galitzian you'd better count your fingers to make sure you got them all back!

Months and months went by. I've already told you how happy and calm I felt for the first time in five years, since I left my home, actually. We celebrated weddings and other events. I remember most fondly when we gathered to accompany our first thirteen year old at his Bar Mitzvah. Son of my dear wise and humble friend Kalman Sabludovski, arrived as a child with his parents, a skinny eleven year old. Now we rejoiced on his Sacred Birthday which made him responsible for his own actions before god. He was welcomed by the group to receive the honor of reading Torah, the Five Books of Moses. I'm telling you, we hugged and hugged him with Mazel Tov's!

There was a lot of partying. We had honey cake and wine at the decorated house of the Sabludovskis. When I saw little Leo put on his tallis and his phylacteries on his left arm and forehead, proclaiming the divine order of "a sign on your arm and a remembrance between your eyes," Lendov appeared before me. Nu? Not surprised, are you?

Weddings were something else. I would get so excited and happy I even danced on tables, with my inseparable companion in my arms, my banjo.

She's so depressed. No wonder they say Venezuela is Caracas, period. It wasn't that Caracas was a great metropolis nor that Valencia was a desert, but there was something very dry, a certain aridity in this city of so much history and in its present makeup of tall buildings and well-stocked supermarkets. From the outside, to the newly arrived, Valencia seemed like an acceptable bridge between the urban and the rural. In daily life one could see the light years that separated it from the relative cosmopolitanism of Caracas. The capital, at least, offered the possibility of a good concert at the Teatro Municipal, select films at the Bellas Artes, a play at the Teatro Nacional, and maybe some decent popular music at the Hipopótamo: middle-class pleasures which seemed impossible to give up.

What could this unusual young couple do on a Valencian Sunday afternoon? They didn't play dominoes, nor the local bolas ball game. They didn't bet on the lottery, nor on the five and six horse races. They didn't drink anything, not even beer. No wonder it was difficult for them to meet new people in this society, or any other society for that matter. They were unhappy with the silent rejection they seemed to earn because they did not share pork cookouts, baptisms, and communions. But they kept reminding themselves and repeating to each other that they were here, teaching, and doing it for the good of their country.

There was no chance of a group catharsis because that lovely congregation of street peddlers, to which her father had belonged, and which at one time had made Valencia a model of communal adjustment had disappeared, completely integrated into Caracas.

Civilization versus barbarism? Hardly. It was simply and painfully just a question of customs. There were some interesting ruins. They discovered one quite by accident one Sunday afternoon in the Bárbula Psychiatric Colony: Matitiaju Roitman.

While fulfilling a promise she had made her father, a bothersome duty of visiting a crazy schizophrenic young man turned into a warm and informative encounter. Matias, as he was called, was the sanest person in the sanatorium so he was in charge of guarding, like a permanent guarding nurse. He spoke of his mother and sisters who with severe punctuality sent letters from Argentina, where they had lived for the past twenty years.

And it was Matias who introduced them to Berta Krakoski, a plump old lady with very curly, dyed red hair. Her obvious flirting couldn't hide the melancholy mood she was in.

"Friends, here's the Madame, a person of our religion and practically my mother." When she heard our names she became excited, as if she were back in some private limbo. She closed her eyes saying:

"Oy yoy yoy. I knew them all well. You hear me? All the men of our colony here in Valencia. Oy yoy yoy! I left Bucovina when I was still a little girl, to work as a ironing maid. But one of our bastards, a real shit, sold me to another one of ours, who traffic in white women to Buenos Aires and Lima. Fleeing from him, I got to Venezuela with a friend who was coming to get married. Anyway, what did I know how to do? Nothing! Just lie down and wait for them to arrive. One after the other. Oy yoy yoy! But I was very clean, you know? I would wash with vinegar before and after each one and because of that I was always the prettiest and the favorite at El Morro. . . . Want to know something? I was never with Gentiles. I kept on being the hidden girlfriend of all my fellow Jews, before and after they got married . . . but I was never invited to a wedding, nor to a Bris. Never even knew when they had Bar Mitzvahs . . . Oy yoy yoy! And I swear to you, I've always fasted on Yom Kippur. . . ."

Matias dries her tears tenderly with a filthy handkerchief and leads her softly and solicitously toward the white building, greeting us with a "Come back soon!" ❖

Rosa Krieger has a welcoming restaurant on Colombia Street. Sometimes it happens that while her husband takes care of the dinners, she sings our melodies on a broken-down piano in the back of the room.

One Saturday noon the sour pickles look appetizing but lunch turns out to be flavorless because I need the company of a woman and Rosa's music adds only tears to my vegetable soup. Even the tastiest dish has no flavor unless you can share it with someone you love.

Rakovich and his wife Esther arrive. She is majestic, and even though very young, has a bit of grey in her hair. I have heard about her. She is the center of all the gossip among my friend's wives, the only one who works outside the home, and without her husband. I'm sure you can imagine what else they said. . . .

They ask if they can take the empty seats at my table.

"It's a great honor to eat with you."

"How are you?"

"Alright, I guess."

"Are you ill?"

"God forbid, my dear lady. Why do you ask?"

"Your eyes are red."

"Ay, just a little homesickness, nothing else."

"Thank heavens. It's just that I'm a nurse and there is so much typhus here and so I thought . . ."

"Oy, no no no. God forbid."

"Anyway, since you're a greenhorn in this part of the country, take care not to be bitten by flies and mosquitos. You should sleep with a mosquito net. If you feel feverish or have chills, don't be embarrassed, let me know and I'll give you a shot of some special medicine for those symptoms."

I didn't want to interrupt her, but I had already seen malaria attacks among my customers in Valencia and Caracas. Also, among us, we used to say that some little towns like Parapara and Ortiz had almost completely disappeared as their inhabitants fell, one after the other, just like during the plagues in the days of the Pharaohs. And what did the government do? Nothing, absolutely nothing!

"I'm sure you know, my friend, that my wife studied first aid with the Red Cross in Rovno during the Great War."

"It's true. Here I teach the midwives to use a lot of alcohol to disinfect. I concentrate on the San Blas Parish and believe me, I've got enough work."

"You mean they don't use alcohol?"

"Not always! Can you believe that? When I go to the houses of the tubercular to beg them to remain isolated from the others, they set the dogs out on me. I've got to be ready to run like an athlete."

Of course it was not ideal dinner conversation, but Esther spoke with such authority and her desire to help me was so noble that I let her finish and even asked: "One thing I do feel is that my teeth are in bad shape. They fall and break. My gums hurt and bleed. Is there something you could suggest?"

"It's the water here in the Tropics. Drink only filtered water. Also, drink as much boiled milk as you can afford."

"Follow my wife's instructions, young man."

"Gladly, but you know that everything is harder here."

"Don't complain, my friend. Valencia is Paradise compared to Maracaibo. There we got our water out of wells full of snakes and frogs."

"I can't believe that. Not even in my poor little village had I heard of that!"

"I'm not lying. The children fetch and drink that water daily and their stomachs are bigger than they are because they're full of live worms."

"Oy yoy yoy! The poor children! What suffering!"

"In Caracas I was a peddler on a mule. Here I travel by trolley like a gentleman. Let me tell you, Valencia is progress. I repeat, don't complain."

"I believe you . . ."

I heard many tales as I rested in the little parks of Santa Rosa of El Palotal and San Blas near El Morro. Waiting for the afternoon breeze before going back to my room, I would say to myself that I was not so badly off. There were real dramas, some even brought a smile . . . like the one about Steinbach who arrived at Lagunilla in the State of Zulia. Determined to sell wheat bread, he looked for a motor boat and when he didn't find one, he grabbed a *chalana*, a canoe used by the indigenous people, and headed out to the huts on Lake Maracaibo with his sack of breads. The problem was, you see, that the people of that region eat only plantains! The poor man insists. Sometimes he goes at it for three days straight only to return defeated, without a cent with which to feed his wife and two kids. Four mouths swallow that bread, turned into rocks by the humidity. It would be funny if it weren't so painful. . . .

Life was filled with collective duties. We had to visit the Lachbergs, recently arrived, because of all that Love Thy Neighbor stuff. The wife, Miss Sara, is a very cultured, university-trained Rumanian. She speaks a lot with a soprano's voice and smiles beautifully. She has vivacious eyes, but her memories of Europe, which she left to come with Nudel Lachberg, shroud her in a look of permanent grief.

"I don't want my Nudele to keep lowering himself by knocking on doors to sell crucifixes and frames. He's an important and very sensitive Cantor," she says.

"But you have to eat, don't you?"

"Well, yes, of course. That's the only reason I put up with this jungle of barefooted monkeys."

Also, as you know, one must visit the sick and the grieving to alleviate their pain. We did it with Dina Reiner when she gave birth to still-born twins. She had been in Valencia for a year, so absorbed in her Bucharest past and trying to convince her husband of how wrong he was in choosing this place as a home, that she didn't pay attention to the nine months. She began swelling up and thought that it was her liver because of the change of diet and water. Until her neighbor, Miss Ruperta Quiñones, had to run for the midwife and six hours later they heard: "Ma'am, they were twins. . . ."

Ay yay yay. Charming wives. We used to call them "ladies of the park" because they gathered there every afternoon to chat and tell stories while waiting for their husbands, the schleppers to return.

The most romantic love story I ever witnessed happened around that time. The protagonists were a Gentile and one of ours. She, Ana Josefina Olalquiaga, daughter of a good Catholic family, had had a son by a first husband, or was he? It wasn't clear. She had seen better days, as they say of people who suddenly lose their fortune, and her well-cared-for mansion was the rooming house our Albert Blumenfeld landed in when he set foot in Valencia.

Blumenfeld received her passion and protection until her growing stomach announced the landlady's second child. The creature is born and Alberto remains silent. Suddenly, a month later, he shows up at the plaza inviting us to a wedding and Bris, telling us that Ana Josefina was given a ritual bath, in Caracas, and that now she's one of us. "I expect you all tomorrow early." With cheers of some and griping of others, he manages to gather a total of ten males needed to legitimize both ceremonies, the agreement of the spouses, and the pact with god. But even today, Mrs. Rusnak still swears: "I saw her with my own eyes. While they cut the baby's chord, Ana Josefina made the sign of the cross over and over again in the next room before a statue of the Virgin of Coromoto. And how she didn't burn down the house with all the candles she lit that day, I'll never know. The cheat! After converting still doing all that witchcraft."

Nu? Let me tell you something, the love between Alberto and Ana, blessed with a child who's probably already a doctor, maybe a lawyer, lasted until both their deaths. They were a close and loving couple to the end.

All this was going on while we sweated the sales of more and more rags. We got the merchandise from the wholesalers who were Christian Arabs: the Turiks, the Alfon, the Mocci, the Nao who were our business cousins. Sound friendships united us always. Those Lebanese Turks were very successful because they supplied the retailers and peddlers of La Victoria, Tinaquillo, and the surrounding Valencia area. Let me tell you, good friendship, yes Siree!

Interesting thing, there never was a love affair but neither was there ever a duel between us and the German colony. They resided almost completely toward Camoruco, in houses built at the end of sumptuous gardens, and in the afternoons, you could see them sitting on the porches, drinking beer. If for example I needed glasses, I'd go to the Opticals Danube of Gunter Branvol, the German, buy what I needed, and "good afternoon." Why? I don't know. It was simply business.

It's impossible to talk about Valencia and not mention the cars. Mrs. Kizer, on foot, in front of her husband's Chevrolet, to "guide him through the curves," she used to say. Never, not even at a Chaplin movie, did I have such a great time. Her commanding yells made it seem like real war! And the other one, Ruterman's wife, cursing him because he didn't shift to third going up on Libertad Street. Her yells could be heard all the way to Camp Carabobo, a place near Valencia, covered with fine grass and full of statues. I was moved before a monument in the shape of an arch, honoring those who liberated Venezuela. The day I saw it, I wrote four stanzas in Yiddish in honor of Simon Bolívar.

One fine day I counted up my savings and it occurred to me that I had enough to stop knocking on doors. I felt tired. After daily expenses, what I send my parents and my widowed sister in Radom, and what I have to save as dowry for my younger sister Reisl, I managed to save twenty thousand bolívares, seven thousand dollars. A pretty impressive sum for a knower of nothing. A schlepper. A knocker on doors. A cláper.I decide to go to Caracas, to get advice from someone in our association on the best way to invest this. I'd rather not remember the farewell my Valencia brothers gave me. . . .

One could tell by the ruins that the Federal High School had once been the mansion of some famous Spaniard.

"The chalk hasn't arrived from Caracas, yet."

"The office has received no instructions on that."

"We're waiting for the Minister's approval to buy the folders."

"Probably next year . . ."

"Yes, they did offer more desks but . . ."

"No, we've never had a library here."

"A copier? My heavens, you've got fancy notions!"

"It must be the heat and your pregnancy that have you so upset."

"My dear young professor, without all those extras you seem to think we need, in the last five years we've graduated four hundred high schoolers for the Republic. You can't deny that that's an impressive victory for our democratic leadership!"

Three hundred and sixty-five days and their nights! Good-bye Valencia. They are returning to the nation's belly. Were any seeds planted in these barren lands? . . . Perhaps some other day. . . . ❖

Vilner had finally settled in Maracay. I stay for a few days with him and his wife, Raquelita Oistrach, on my way back to Caracas. He found a lot of work in the town where Gómez, the Benemérito or Meritorius Saviour of the Nation lives. The city is a beautiful garden, like Versailles, but instead of smelling like roses, it smells like cows. Warmer than Valencia, the only coolness is under the magnificent rain-trees. Packards and Lincolns fitting six government officials circle the city all the time. Samuel laughs as he explains how to pronounce the name. "Listen, Ma-ra-cay: In the Indian tongue it means Tiger. From here, Gómez and his gang control, with very sharp claws, the rest of the country."

In his dark room, at the end of the second patio, and between cameras, moulds, and samples, I see a picture of the Rehabilitator, as he is sometimes called. I'm impressed by the icy, defiant look coming from behind thick eyeglasses. His face is wide and he has a bushy mustache. He's like a Caribbean Stalin, posing in uniform, military cap, chain with loads of medals, and, to the left of his chest, a star, not like ours but an eight-pointed one.

Vilner shows me another one, taken under the Guere rain-tree. Above it you can see the words: Peace, Country, and Work. In this one he looks better, with his gloves on, four pockets with I don't know how many buttons, hat and cane. More paternal.

"Peace in the cemeteries, work on the highways and union in jails, say the barefooted ones."

"Tell me, Sammy, and his wife? what about his wife?"

"Not wife, concubine."

"What, and he takes pictures with her?"

"Of course, this one is the main one."

"Explain, Samuel . . ."

"He never married, but has so many kids that nobody has been able to count them. He makes a bastard with any skirt he feels like. Now they're talking about a beautiful Catalan woman. But this one you see here is almost official, the rich lady from a wealthy family. Understand a little better?"

"Not much, Sammy. But it reminds me of our Simon Horowitz of Valencia. Good friend of Simon Herrera, the priest who wanted to baptize his tree children. Every Saturday he went to the house for lunch and repeated that it was his obligation to put holy water on their heads. Otherwise, the devil himself would carry them away."

"I never heard this one when I was in Valencia. So, nu, what happened?"

"Well, one Saturday our Simon got tired and answered: 'Listen, buddy, we both wear very similar prayer hats right?' "

"With all due respect, my friend, mine is called a solideo or skullcap because it's used only to pray to the Holiest in Churches and Chapels of the Holy Spirit."

"Well, although they look alike, they're not the same and neither are we. I'll let you baptize my children the day you get married, Monsignor."

"Well, this is something like what Gómez is supposed to have answered the Bishop of Caracas when he recommended the marvels of matrimony. 'If it's so great, how come the Pope doesn't marry?' he said. Sharp guy, nu?"

Samuel was an encyclopedia of stories about the dictator but among all the ones he told me at that time, the one that most affected me was the one about his uncountable progeny. I pictured an enormous bull irrigating all the fields of Venezuela with little calves he never knew.

I saw these little "calves" on my way to Caracas. They really did live like animals, barefooted and on dirt floors. Just like in Cuba, these also were unemployed, and just hanging around their mud huts.

The ARC bus driver seems to guess my questions because since I'm seated in the first seat I can hear his sung thoughts:

> *El que nació pa pobre y su signo es niguatero*
> *Aunque le saquen la nigua*
> *Siempre le queda el agujero. . . .*
>
> *If you're born poor and bitten by chiggers*
> *you'll wear the holes if not the fleas.*

Vilner, who's with me on his way to the capitol to buy some materials, tells me that a chigger is like lice. Also, he informs me that all the nation's highways have been built by "shovels and spades, used by imprisoned students and other rebels, shackled to several kilos of iron on each ankle. Oy yoy yoy! And all those lands you see, with tobacco, sugar cane and over there that milk factory and the one further down, a paper factory, all of it, absolutely all of it, belongs to him or was a gift from him to some cohort."

This makes me think of the Polish landowners of my village. They live off our rent in palaces with other princes, far from us. "Listen, Sammy, the man in the pictures seems like a simple farmer, what's he do with all the money?"

"They say he's got more than two hundred million that the Americans have given him for the oil. But you're right. He dresses the same always. Eats little. Doesn't drink, smoke, or dance. Believe me."

"How do you know all that?"

"Haven't I photographed him? And anyway, I hear things when I work at the Hotel Jardín which is always crawling with foreigners and government people who come all the way to Maracay to offer him gifts, letters, and girls. In exchange, they beg for jobs, lands, and other favors. Gómez likes that. . . ."

I love listening, but I beg my friend not to mention the tyrant's name or any places associated with him, because there probably are spies on this very bus.

"Yeah, you're right. Well, as I was saying, it's all about: 'what's in it for me?' They ask him to witness their children's and siblings' weddings. They're real ass kissers! You can spot them right away because they wear dark suits, felt hats; some even wear a tux in the middle of the afternoon! And with all this heat! Imagine! He, always in khakis, with his hand around his cane, as if nothing were happening, always enjoying the party in his honor, but never participating, just watching."

The day before we had visited Nuñe Oldsvang on Pérez Almarza Street, practically next door to Vilner.

"Are you doing well here in Maracay?" I ask.

"I make a living."

He's very angry because he has to deliver several suits to some ministers. Without raising his eyes from his work, he tells us about his comings and goings as a traveling tailor to the big shots:

"If you really want to know the truth, those guys are respectful and quiet. What scares me are other things. Like last Tuesday, I'm walking with my cutting scissors wrapped in a newspaper. I hadn't realized that because they're so long, the part you put your fingers through was sticking out of the wrapping. So, what happens? Right away a policeman spots me and grabs me by the arm:

"Hey, what you got there?"

"See for yourself," I say.

"Why are you carrying that weapon? You know they're forbidden!"

"Weapon? Mr. Policeman, look. What do I have right here behind my lapel?"

"Hmm, I see a needle . . ."

"And here, in my pocket?"

"A thimble."

"Well, these are the weapons of my job. I'm a tailor and I'm taking my scissors to the grinder to be sharpened."

"Hell, you shouldn't be running around with that thing. Get yourself a smaller one or something. Anyone could mistake you for, I mean, even I thought . . . . C'mon *musiuito,* let's grab us some breakfast."

"Good idea! Let's get one of those *arepas* with cheese at my countryman Dov Akerman's place, right around the corner. And don't worry about a thing, it's on me!"

As you see, brothers, all you need is a little mazel!

And Nuñe dries his wrinkled forehead with a piece of cloth.

"Caracas/allí está/ vedla tendida . . . Caracas/there she lies . . . ," wrote the poet Perez Bonalde. . . . For ten years she existed on irregular verbs, subordinate clauses, consonant and dissonant rhymes, Fray Luis, and Santa Teresa, Virgil, and the Chanson de Roland, Tolstoy, A la recherche du temps perdu, Russell and Pygmalion, Kafka, J. L. Borges, Hopscotch *and* Pedro Páramo, *No One Writes to the Colonel,* and Vargas Llosa.

She overwhelmed the students with midterms, weekly evaluations, monthly seminars, and course advising. Was it really really possible to teach literature?

Curricular changes were instituted every five years whether they were needed or not. Slowly, the pleasures of reading literature became nothing more than a rusty tool used to collect a pay check and pay the rent. Would reading for pleasure ever be part of her life again?

Humberto Rodanés, now an important congressman of the new republic, had probably been right. Is her intolerance really a bourgeois trait? She can no longer stand systematic noise and chaos. She's upset by idleness that is rewarded with a salary. She's petrified by those hoodlums dressed like students who keep stirring social resentment.

She trembles at strike orders that come from malnourished young leaders.

Would obeying this disorder make her a good citizen? Will all this ferment of meetings, strikes, tire burning, lifting of constitutional rights, take-overs, signed agreements, kidnapping of officials, reopening of schools, and new strikes be the educational constitution that rules the country in the near future? Should she try to adapt her personality and change it, or should she follow her impulse to quit and find another profession?

She's disoriented. Things aren't right or is it she who has become disaffected with the system? Those who know her say it's her need for perfection. In any event, there is a breakdown somewhere. But, is it irreversible?

"That's why I came to this first and very costly consultation, doctor. They told me you were a serious psychoanalyst. Can someone who deals with the craziness of the human mind be serious? Well, please forgive me if I offended you. . . . Look, Doctor, before beginning and if I'm treatable, please read this poem by Rafael Cadenas:

> *Yo que no soy lo que soy*
> *que ha pesar de todo tengo un orgullo satánico*
> *aunque a ciertas horas haya sido humilde*
> *hasta igualarme a las piedras. . . .*
>
> *I who am not what I am*
> *who in spite of everything possesses satanic pride*
> *which at times*
> *makes me humble enough to think myself a stone. . . .*

Yes, yes, please read on. It's called "Defeat" and it might serve as an introduction to . . . ❖

In Caracas, for the second time, I do what those in the know tell me. I set up shop in the downtown area at San Jacinto and Traposos. I don't "clap" on any doors. Enough of that. I buy merchandise wholesale and sell it retail in my little shop, "The Bargain Corner," near the main market, practically across the street from the house in which Simon Bolívar was born.

The center of the market is called a beach and is an enormous fair full of stalls and bars where they sell cheap booze, a penny a shot, with funny names like "donkey and buzzard's juice." I can't stand the flavor of the stuff nor do I want to like it because I often see how alcohol drives a man away from his family. I prefer lemonade, something called *chicha* made of rice and plain soda. You know? I can't bear the smell of pig's intestines, yellow corn, tomatoes, carite fish, and the cheap wine of Las Palmas, mixed with the smell of manure. Around here everything—meat, fish, and fruit—everything arrives on donkeys, mules, and horses.

One morning, a crowd assembles a couple of blocks away. Two ladies and one gentleman get out of a car. They buy toucan parrots, thrushes, blue jays, and other birds. After paying, they open the cages and let the birds fly away. The children applaud enthusiastically. The captive creatures are now free. Seems this is an agency that protects animals, but you should have seen the envy in the onlookers eyes. At least it seemed that way to me. And all day long, my buyers would say, almost in a whisper: "Did you see how high they flew?" "They looked so happy!"

Nearby at Las Gradillas, there is a well-supplied gadget store, "The Pretty One," owned by the fat and jovial Amador Benabí. He and I become close friends. Friends? Like the tango:

Los amigos ya no vi-e-nen
ni siquiera a visita-rme
Nadie quiere consol-ar-me. . . .

Friends no longer come
not even to visit
no one can console me in my loneliness. . . .

Some friends have drifted away from their old rooming-house buddies, mostly because success seems to poison, even without biting. Maybe that's why I appreciate this Turkish brother and his Fermosa, whom he married last year in Morocco and who now is a seamstress right at the store.

"Shalom, my friend."

"May peace be with you too, my friend. You know something? The guy who just walked out of here said he had met my father in Caucagua, nearly a quarter of a century ago. Imagine that! My father had bought some land and wanted to grow cocoa."

"What did he do with the cocoa?"

"He stored it and traded between here and there."

"What do you mean?"

"Well, he would get fish and brown sugar from a guy in Capaya and give him cocoa. Then he would give what he had gotten to another in exchange for coffee and beans, you get it? Or sometimes, from here they would send him barrels of wine, cheeses, olives, and candies and he would pay for it in coffee beans and the same cocoa shipped from Carenero."

"And was it profitable?"

"Very. So much so that ten years later he went back home and married Sol Corcias, a young lady who knew French, embroidered, painted, and had been a teacher in Tetuan. Momma arrived with all her energy and took over the accounting. She also taught at the rural school in the Pantoja neighborhood, near Caucagua.

In the middle of our chat, in walks Marcos Levy, another Sephardy. He owns Rey Shoes. We invite him to join us since it is twenty to two, which is closing time anyway. He is the nephew of Rafael Mizrachi, who together with old man Nessim Benabí made it in America, in the state of Miranda.

"My father used to say that there were six families there. Right, Amador?"

"That's right. The Toledanos, the Mizrachi, the Esayags, the Bendayans, the Obadias, and us. The Christians called all of us Moroccans!"

"And how did you manage the prayers and stuff like that?"

"Right in my house. For Sukkot, we would make sheds in the back yard, with our neighbor's help in fact. They sang our hymns with us waving branches of the four holy species. Since we had no cider or myrtle nor willow, we just waved palm leaves and would imagine the rest! On Pesach, those same Christians would help us look for the pieces of matzoh wrapped in paper that Poppa had hidden. After they were found, he would burn them, saying a special prayer to begin the wheat fast which would last eight days. At the end, on the night of Mimuna, all together we would stuff ourselves on milk, honey, and lots of flour and yeast foods."

"Yes, I remember everything Amador is telling you because I was about five at the time. Pesach was so delicious over there that my Father preferred to go all the way to his brother's house in Caucagua than stay here in Caracas."

"So, you never had any problems because of your different customs?"

"None whatsoever, my friend."

"You were lucky, because in Poland, or in Cuba, it isn't so pleasant."

"Of course, in order to have me circumcized, they had to take me by canoe to Santa Teresa del Tuy and from there all the way here on horseback, so that they could have a real Bris, there was no other way."

"And what did your mother do?"

"Well, I'll tell you. She was so committed to educating the children that she would go every morning, with a policeman, from door to door, picking them up for school. She really did that! Can you believe it? Since the parents were peasants, they thought she wanted them to work in the fields."

"Boy, what character!"

"And let me tell you, she did all of that and raised four children who arrived one right after the other too."

"And, what about your father?"

"Well, he helped her. He collected signatures from door to door to demand that the government add two more years to primary education. You see the boys and the girls school went only up to fourth grade. Both my parents became teachers of the people, in every sense of the word. They also taught by example: how to eat vegetables, to boil milk and water, to take daily baths and to maintain personal hygiene, how to use all parts of the cow, let me tell you, they succeeded against incredible odds!"

Time has come to reopen the stores, but Benabí invites me to hear the rest of the story. "Come have Shabbat dinner with us tomorrow night and I'll show you some books and pictures that will interest you."

Was there a more meaningful mission in life than to be a teacher?

Yes, she had always had an educator's vocation, ever since she was a little girl. But these results were troubling. If out of forty pupils, which was the class average, fifteen fail and the rest pass with the minimum grade, shouldn't it be looked into very carefully? And whose failure is that anyway? Isn't it as serious if it happens to the children of the "nobodies" down there in the Lidici neighborhood as if it happens in the Prados del Este to the children of the "somebodies?" It must be her. She's just not good at this. . . .

Ah language! It communicates and motivates personal experiences. And to teach it! God, she adores the profession. So why does this government, which overcame so many political obstacles, persist in subsidizing an educational system that is expensive and totally irrelevant to the real needs of its constituents? Why does this convulsive reprogramming go on? Why the hell do we insist on producing illiterate graduates out of these chronically malnourished, fatherless, familyless, and homeless creatures? Why do they lie to them and turn them out with titles but without the means of earning a living? Why does the administration get bigger and bigger and set up more and more boards every five years during party elections? Why is the department in charge of educating Venezuelans an office full of militants? Is she the only one bothered by this? She doesn't feel well. Imprisoned. An alien. A cockroach at a hens' party. . . .

She must have failed at the job. Could this pessimistic vision be the result of a long-endured and hopeless neurosis, Doctor? She must go deeper. ❖

Six o'clock, Friday. In honor of Sabbath, I put on my best clothes. The Benabís live in the El Conde district. As I told you before, I like Amador very much. He is not like any of those who forget how miserable they were yesterday and as soon as they get rich show off their fancy dining room saying: "On this oak table we can feed—god forbid!—up to thirty. . . ."

Quite the opposite. After all the "Shabbat Shalom! A git shabbos!" I notice that almost all their guests are humble Greek and Moroccan peddlers. Amador shows each guest the same respect and, with great pride, introduces his mother, a small and fragile old lady, whose appearance seems to negate the incredible vigor of her biography: "This is our Sun!" he says, which is what her name means in Spanish. I shudder before the son's sentence. I'm so envious. Oy Mommala! . . .

It is when she speaks that Mrs. Sol shows her real strength.

"Don't you think for a moment that my husband Nessim, may he rest in peace, was anybody's fool! We had heard about a group of women and children who in the 1800s landed in Puerto Cabello seeking asylum after the French invaded Curaçao. So, the Spanish governor asked the Real Audiencia whether he should let them stay. And do you know what the bastards answered? They answered no. The Real Audiencia said that local inhabitants had to be protected against the contagion of that religion."

"Mrs. Sol, many Polish Catholics still think that, even today."

"Yes, unfortunately, it's a centuries' old disease."

"It seems to me that if Mr. Nessim bought land, as your son told me, he must have felt pretty secure here. Is that why he decided to stay the moment he arrived?"

"That's true, dear guest. He was from Spanish Morocco and had no language problems. He was more afraid of the fanatical Arab tribes of his homeland. That's why he felt comfortable here. He didn't feel threatened and went so far as to put his children in the school of the Sacred Heart of Jesus. Of course, they did not attend Catechism classes. Our own liturgy is sacred to us and we're very careful not to lose even one of our traditions. Look, I'd rather use red vinegar and water rather than profane liquor when we have no Kosher wine."

Among the dinner guests, there is also an older peddler born in Salonica by the name of Jacobo Gallemus who tells wonderful tales of his adventures. He is very erudite and knows a lot about the history of his countrymen in Venezuela.

"Did you know that our brothers from Curaçao and the Antilles came through Coro and helped Bolívar a lot?"

"Don Jacobo, those must be made up stories."

"No, not at all, my friend. You can find them in the history books. A Benjamín Henríquez was cavalry captain, another Isidoro Barowski, probably Russian, was a famous soldier. Then there was an Isaac de Sola born in St. Thomas who reached the rank of colonel and fought with the Battalion of Apure's Brave Men at the battle of Carabobo."

"Oh yeah, that battlefield right outside of Valencia, I've been there."

"Let me tell you, young man, that was the glorious battle that gave Venezuela its freedom. There's more. When Bolívar and Miranda failed at the first republic, they were still very young. They fled to Curaçao. And who do you think took care of them just like a father? Well, none other than Doctor Mordechai Ricardo, that's who. There is a letter of thanks to him from Bolívar. Not only that, but there is more than one rumor about Field Marshall Antonio José de Sucre being a descendant of conversos."

When the other guests leave, Benabí takes me to his library and opens a voluminous book that's on his desk.

"If you read Spanish well, I would lend you this jewel that I found last year on my trip to Spain and Africa. You would faint if you found out what Simon Rodríguez, Bolívar's famous teacher, said about the hypocrisy of the Europeans. And, about Russia, Poland, and Turkey with their millions of slaves and their contempt for our fellow Jews."

"Veis meir! And so long ago?"

"Less than a hundred years, actually. And, look here, the wise man says that America should not imitate those 'inferior' powers but should be original and start fresh."

"And do you think, my friend, that America is different?"

"The Spaniards who conquered and colonized were not. They were Catholics directed by the Inquisition. But the mestizos, today's Americans, are liberal, fun loving, and well meaning, at least the ones around here. They never stick their noses in anyone else's pot. My mother Sol, whom you just met, used to sing while she cooked and knitted. Some of the words would keep me up late at night when I was a child. One of them was

Pienso y digo
qué va a ser de mí
en tierras ajenas
no se puede vivir. . . .

I wonder to myself
what will become of me
in someone else's land
I cannot live. . . .

That night, in bed, while I wait for my soul to leave my body, I begin to understand how it is that my Turkish brothers can think of this country as their ancient crib.

The main office is frigid and so is her attitude. Soledad Vásquez de Maldonado, grim-faced, well-dressed matron, Chair.

"I am very sorry to have to tell you, esteemed professor, that the report by the ministry's supervisor has several complaints about your behavior in the classroom."

"Really? What did I do?"

"In his presence, you confused a circumstantial complement with an adverb, grammatical with syntactical analysis."

"Heavens! I'm in trouble. Even sicker than I thought."

"Furthermore, he states that you are quite incapable of maintaining discipline. Your students seems to have a lot of discussions and you don't seem to be able to control them enough to actually cover the material you're supposed to."

"Well, that part is true. I never used my position to control anybody. On the contrary, I actually try to take advantage of its creative potential to excite. On one thing I have been strict, without much help from you I might add, in demanding that the students themselves keep the classroom clean, because if they get used to filthy classrooms, waiting for a janitor to clean, then they won't be upset by their dirty country. Filthy in the broadest sense of the word. You know what I mean?"

"It's not too late to mend your ways. The next evaluation will be in April."

Her first instinct was to find some independent official to take her side, someone strong and with authority. Now there's a rare specimen! Almost extinct around here in fact. . . .

She loved her country deeply, maybe out of gratitude because it had been her father's refuge during the Gómez years and her mother's after the Gómez years. . . . And yet, is mediocrity, as a system, really a patriotic obligation?

"So, Doctor, I quit."

Back in Caracas this time things go pretty well. My clientele is made up mostly of people from San José, Prado de Maria, and the Cemetery neighborhoods. Which reminds me, a small group of us peddlers buy a plot promising the authorities that it will be for a family pantheon but really, it's for all of us. Although we're all still young, we want to make sure to be united in death as we are in life. On this, there's no argument.

Yes sir, my clientele comes from all different parishes. They come from Altagracia, Santa Rosalía, and Barrio Obrero. Oy, "neighborhood" or barrio is a word closely tied to my wakefulness . . . as the tango says:

Lejana tierra mía
de mis amores
Cómo te nombro
en mil noches sin sueño. . . .

Far away land of my loves
I hold you close
in thousands of sleepless nights. . . .

My sleeplessness gets worse every time I see one of those soldiers, those "Saviors" and "Modern War Colossus" go by in their Prussian-cut jackets. Street names like Danger, Dead Men, Black Cat, Misery, Buzzards don't help my state of mind and, to top it off, when I get back to my rooming house, the one between Laguno and Piñango, all I hear is whispers about a den of iniquity called La Rotunda, where they torture enemies of the Never Vanquished One, as the radio calls Gómez. Poor devils, they're forced to endure heavy shackles that make it impossible for them to move, and sleep on the floor next to the real crazies. We hear that many of them have been brutally tortured in their male parts. Nu? Can you see what's bothering me?

I dream of sharp knives; of Mr. Warren's smile turned into a grimace; of lion's teeth and of Liborio Martinez bathed in a crimson liquid. When I wake up, I wonder, am I to blame for what's happening? Can I stop any of this craziness? What good is it for me to spend all my time petrified? About as useful as applying cold compresses to a dead man. So, let's move on, I say to myself. Did I come to work or to tremble? And Gómez? What about Gómez? May he walk on his hands for as long as he walked on his legs, and the rest of the time, he should only get around on his rump! And, may he be the owner of ten shiploads of gold and may he spend it all on doctors!

Now I feel lighter and ready to leave for work.

My sleeping I do at Doña Gumersinda Torres's, but my eating I do entirely at Baruch and Eva Sheindel's restaurant. They and their children are from Yedenitz, which is just like Lendov, only in Bessarabia.

Their restaurant is a big house on the corner of Pedrera and Romualda streets. Sometimes, travelers from the interior stay over night because it also has rooms. More than to eat, what we really go for is to talk. Now we've turned the place into a repository of confessions as well as packages for merchants in a hurry. All this under the imposing presence of mild-mannered Mr. Baruch who, in his patriarchal manner, constantly encourages us: "Everything will be fine, boys. Don't worry so much!"

I meet countrymen working in Barquisimeto, Maracaibo, Mérida, San Cristóbal, and Villa de Cura. "Why does one of us have to live in the village of a priest?"

"Don't be silly. Villa del Cura is just the name of the town. There aren't really any priests there. It's a centrally located area where the ranchers bring their livestock to be sold. It's like a crossroads for cattle ranchers, just like Tinaquillo. So, what happens is that they all have money and are ready to buy anything we offer them. It's what they call a commercial center."

"And why do so many live in Coro when they say it's so dry and full of goats?"

"Listen, for your information, Coro was the very first place our Turkish brothers landed. The Curiels, Capriles, Lopez Fonsecas, Maduros all the way from Curaçao. Understand?"

"Yes, Benabí mentioned that, but you never see one of us. . . ."

"Well, that was about fifty or more years ago. They started everything you can imagine. The first drugstore in the city, the first soap factory, candle, food cans, cigarette, ice, and matches factories. You name it, they started it."

"How come you know so much about it?"

"That's where I work!"

"Since when?"

"I got here two years ago and then I sent for my wife. My name is Menashe Yavner. I'm very pleased to meet you and please, come and visit us whenever you'd like."

When I hear his last name I think of Noaj, the best bricklayer in Lendov. But after a few minutes I realize they're not related because this Menashe comes from Kiev. And yet, only god knows . . . our world is so small.

"So, all those businessmen you've mentioned before are by now a united and helping society, no?"

"Actually, no. They and their children assimilated, marrying Gentiles. What they do have is a beautiful cemetery, may we never need it. The marble gravestones have no crosses, just statues of angels, indicating birth and death dates. But they have no Hebrew letters either. Know what I mean?"

"I'm trying . . ."

"They are De Lima, Chumaceiro, Senior, Correa. Venezuelans of ancestors just like ours but nothing else. Now we are arriving from Russia, Poland, Lithuania, and we are Graterman, Liebson, Bronstein, Samberg. Is it really so hard for you to see the difference?"

At the end of the day, these meetings and chats relax me. But, deep into the night, when some neighbor sings,

Hicieron preso a tu marido, Guillermina
y lo metieron en una fuerte prisión.
Murió mi madre, yo estoy ausente
yo no la vi
pero dice mi padre que en su agonía de muerte
alzó la mano y me bendijo a mí. . . .

They arrested your husband Guillermina
and stuck him in a mean jail.
Mamma died without me
but my father says that on her deathbed
she raised her hand and blessed me. . . .

I can't stop crying.

Yes, my Mommala prays for me too . . . she was the only one who understood and accepted . . . a mother understands even what a son does not say. . . .

There're about two hundred of us now in Caracas, between Poles and Russians. Still, one feels lonely. False friends, like migrating birds, fly away in cold times. Of course I don't reject my circle of friends because I know that to retreat from society only leads to worse things. But I don't always follow them nor do I let them lead me. Some already got too chummy with the green poker tables. I need to be alone at times. I need to put together the pieces of a puzzle that has too many missing pieces and threatens to destroy me if I don't put it in order.

Looking for peace and quiet, I walk along the Los Caobos woods where the silence is occasionally interrupted by the latest model Nash heading very slowly toward the east end of town.

Once I went into the Donzella Brewery, at the corner of Principal and Conde, but there is too much noise at the bar. Carefully I approach the quieter bar in the Majestic Hotel and I have a beer. It's the excuse I use to go in and to find out all the news tourists bring from the North and from Europe.

If dirt you are and to dirt you will return, in the middle, could one little drink really be so bad?

Fumar es un place-r
Geni-aal, sen-su-aal
Fum-ando espero
Al hombre que yo qui-ero
Tras los cristales de alegres venta-na-les
Y mientras fu-mo
Mi vida no con-su-mo
Porque flotan-do el humo
Me suele ador-me-cer. . . .

Smoking is so sen-sual and plea-sure-able
While smo-oking I wa-ait for my lo-over
Behind the shiny glass win-dows
And while smoking my li-fe is suspen-ded
Because the vapors intoxicate me so-o.

Why, if she really wanted to share reading experiences, didn't she ever join one of the literary circles?

Margot Roisenthul, so brilliant and articulate, became the star of the Sortario group and Luna Benchetrit, the toast of the famous intellectual Piso del Tiburón group. And she, who loved the same authors, Vicente Gerbasi, Juan Sanchez Peláez, and Guillermo Meneses and had devoured Jean Cocteau, Albert Camus, Virginia Woolf, Eugene Ionesco, and Simone de Beauvoir, she was unable to stomach these local poetry and prose luminaries for as much as ten minutes.

She liked them privately. After all, they shared close personal ties going all the way back to their university days and literary events. But when she tried to follow them in their Bohemian life styles, their constant pleasure in alcohol, that self-possessed air that pervaded their rhetoric, a schism developed between them.

"Yes, Doctor, as a child, I spent a great deal of time in the care of neighbors. The ones next door were the wonderful Lujan family. The father, attentive Mr. Ramón Emilio, was an efficient hardware store worker. Every Xmas he gave me a present just like the ones he gave his own children. He was always concerned about my needs because "the little Turkish girl is abandoned from sun up to sunset by her foreign working parents," he would say. I spend many days of my childhood in their warm and welcoming home.

But Friday nights and Saturdays, that quiet man disappeared into the corner bar and would return vanquished by alcohol, holding on to his older son Rigoberto's arm. We could hear the cries of his wife Isabela and the children all the way to our house as the possessed man beat them up with his fists. As I grew up, that duality became intolerable and I began to reject his gifts and even his overly courteous weekly greetings. Later we found out that he had two other women on the side with a sizeable progeny in Higuerote and Charallave suburbs of Caracas.

Two completely opposite people in the same body. I feared and distrusted him. In this contradictory friend who claimed to protect her, which of his two extremes was acting? Was it the good and sober one? Was it the drunken evil one?

I suppose, Doctor, you'll probably say that this trauma led to my instinctive rejection of men who drink. . . . A drunkard in bed? Yuck! Bed? Not even at the table. . . . ❖

They caught me by surprise. By the time I turned they were already inside the store. Three of them in white uniforms with wide-brimmed Mexican hats and rifles. They turn over drawers and display windows. Open closets. Check out the bathroom and even look inside my tea thermos. They look threatening. The only sound they make is to ask for identification papers. As they leave one of them says: "Hey, musiú, it's just a *jurungo.*"

I lock up right away and, under the curious gaze of neighbors and passersby, run to Amador the Turk: "Jurungo, my foot," he says. They're *chácharos,* you know, stoolies of the Andean Guards. Listen, *jurungar* means to bother, to upset, and it's used to refer to all of us since peddlers are such pests, which you know better than I because you used to be one yourself. If someone says 'musiú no jurungues,' it's probably because you're charging them too much. Know what I mean? It's just like when someone owes money, they say he's got a Turk on his back, Nu? So what else is new? I've got a customer in Tovar who calls me Mr. Jurungo, which is like saying Mr. Pest! Don't worry so much, my friend. Get a good night's sleep, open your store, and don't 'jurungues' yourself so much!"

Silencio en la noche
Ya todo está en calma
el músculo duerme
la ambición descansa. . . .

Night's quiet
all is calm
muscles sleep
ambition rests. . . .

Since I set foot in this country, one very special voice together with Poppa's and Hershele's has been by my side. The electrical miracle of radio has helped me in my loneliness and through some pretty rough times. When I got back to Caracas, the first thing I did was buy myself an RCA Victor victrola and several records; that way I could hear my new friend, Carlos Gardel, any time I felt like it.

A couple of weeks after the grand opening of my little store, new movies arrived starring my invisible shadow. I reserve tickets in advance and ask my friend Nathaniel Mailberg—a good man who I met in Sheindel's rooming house—to come with me. He told me that while on horseback, from hacienda to hacienda, selling cloth in Armenia,

Colombia, for ten years, he would always listen to Gardel. In fact, he told me, "At night, every station, like clock work, plays Gardel's records to a devout audience of masters, young ladies and gentlemen and all their servants."

But Nathaniel is in love with Talia, one of Sheindel's daughters, who is too young to go to the movies and only knows him as one of the many customers of their restaurant. So, I go with myself. . . .

Let me tell you, there is some pretty great music in *Cuesta Abajo, Luces de Buenos Aires,* and *Melodía de Arrabal,* but the lyrics aren't anything to write home about. I know, I've been composing songs and poems since I was a little boy. Of course I couldn't make a living at it, so I filed them away in my brain. A couple of lucky verses did make it all the way to the *Forward* in New York though. . . . Anyway, it pleases me very much that this guy, this Carlos Gardel, can earn a living with all these tangos he invents and sings. Tell you the truth, that's the one job in the whole world I'd love to have.

That whole year, my existence was tied to Gardel's because he came to Caracas, in person, from Puerto Rico on his way to Colombia. When Caracas Broadcasting advertised his next arrival, I got moving as if someone had announced the Messiah. I bought six-bolívar tickets to the Teatro Principal. It was the first luxury I allowed myself in America.

I sit just a few meters from the stage where they have put a great big flower vase full of flowers. Carlitos seems bald compared to the abundant black hair of his photos and movies. Also, he seems a little fat, not quite as trim as in the movies. In fact, he looks a little ridiculous and effeminate with makeup and powder all over his face, sausaged into a pair of black toreador pants full of red ornaments and long shiny boots.

His three guitarists let out the first chords of

> *Arrastré por este mundo*
> *la verguenza de haber sido*
> *y el dolor de ya no se-er. . . .*

Y crucé por los caminos como un paria
que el destino se empeñó des-ha-cer
si fui ciego si fui flojo. . . .

I dragged myself around the world
with the shame of having been
and the pain of no longer being.
like an outcast, des-ti-ny chose to undo
If I was blind
if I was careless. . . .

Gottenyu, I'm so grateful Nathaniel didn't come this time either. I wouldn't have wanted him to see my tears. The fact is I envy Carlitos's power to sing so artfully, and in public yet, what I, guiltily and dreamily think of in bed

sueño
con el pasado que añoro
y que nunca volverá
Volver. . . .

I dream
of the past I so long for
and which never can return
return. . . .

In powerful lyrics, this odd young man says some pretty terrible truths that his generation relates to easily. . . .

Si tienes en tu mano la verdad
ya nadie te podrá a tí cambiar
conocerás mejor a la gente
y actuarás siempre de frente
porque ellos, algún día
así lo harán.
Libera pues tu mente ya

no bajes más la frente, no
ve siempre hacia adelante
nunca atrás.

If you hold truth in your hand
No one will ever change you
You'll know people better
You'll always act truthfully
And some day so will they.
Free your mind
Don't lower your brow
Always go forward
Never back. . . .

Disenchantment, yearning for openness, a quest for authenticity. Everything, in fact, that the culture, in the Baroque key of its pedantic hermetism, did not share with the masses, can be found in Trino Mora's songs.

I say this here, within the four walls of your office, Doctor, because if I were to be honest, and say this among my intellectual friends, they would call me vulgar. They're really cultured. They prefer the latest London Philharmonic recording of Beethoven.

I love classical music too. I particularly enjoy Chopin and Brahms, and among the Venezuelans, I adore Juan Bautista Plaza. He had been my music teacher at the Academy of Music, when it was near the Rome Theater and where I was always his main diva at all the performances. And let's not forget the two Antonios: Estévez and Lauro, for them I'd give up sleeping altogether! But the popular songs of this restless, young generation appeal to me very much, and at times I think they're darn good literature. The lyrics accurately depict the terrible state the country their parents and grandparents are bequeathing them is really in.

You know, Doctor, you can't talk about these things just anywhere. . . . ❖

Ever since the "Sacred Ones" searched my place, I close earlier. I go straight to the Sheindel's to eat and from there straight to my room to read *The Sphere* or the *New Daily* or any other newspaper guests might leave on one of Mrs. Gumer's straw chairs, the ones she watches over as if there were velvet or something. Only on Saturdays do I go visiting and chatting.

My countrymen play dominoes and cards. Me? I can't. Cards and table games never interested me so I never learned to play them. I just read and read. A magazine, some Yiddish book. And I have a new hidden vice: every Thursday at 8:30 sharp I tune in Broadcasting Radio and enjoy thirty minutes of friendly fights with the Santa Teresa radio show. It helps me increase my vocabulary and makes me laugh, which is more than I can say for some of the jokes I hear around here. Like the one about the two guys who were plotting Stalin's assassination. They found out that he would go to the same place every day at the same time. Armed with pistols, they await at the appointed time. Minutes pass. No Stalin. Still they wait. Hours pass. No Stalin. They wait. When it gets dark, finally one says to the other: "Boy, I hope nothing happened to him!" You should see how they laugh. But me? How can I enjoy such failure? The fact that they don't kill Stalin disappoints me too much.

Now I sleep better because Pacheco arrived. Who's Pacheco, you ask? The cold weather. They call it Pacheco because a Spaniard from the islands, Francisco Pacheco, years ago used to bring the most beautiful flowers from the hills of Galipan on these December days. Here at the rooming house, near La Pastora, the most elevated part of town, almost at the foot of Mount Avila, the cold hits even harder, almost like a European autumn.

Lejana tierra mía
bajo tu cielo
quiero morirme un día. . . .

Far off land of mine
under your sky and
in your embrace
I want to die someday. . . .

It's a national holiday, the anniversary of the Liberator's death. I take advantage of the free time to write home in the midst of troubling rumors about the dictator's health.

At dawn, Mrs. Gumer knocks loudly on all the doors. Excitedly she yells: "Gentlemen, General Gómez died. May God keep him in his glory! For sure there will be a blood bath now!"

Everyone runs to look out on the street between the curtains that cover the large living room windows and I turn on the big radio in the dining room, to hear the news. The owner goes looking for her friends and comes back crossing herself. "They say he died a few minutes before midnight . . . they say he refused extreme unction! . . . No, not the priest, and that he said . . ."

Should I read the Bible more? Take religion more seriously and not just as something that differentiates me from others? Probably.

Take a look at my parents. Poppa never allowed us to suffer through a full day of fasting on Yom Kippur and Momma started lighting Friday night candles when I was fifteen. So what? Either of them have an identity conflict? I hate that pompous-sounding phase! But really, I can't ever imagine either one of them asking "Who am I?" "Where do I come from?"

I do however. I really should study more carefully the history of the people they bequeath me in my genes, without consulting me, I might add. At least I should know: What happened? What is happening? What will happen? Then I'll have the right to decide whether it's a question of god, the evil devil, mine, or of all of the above.

Since I was given a centuries-old tradition, maybe I should get to know it a little better. Maybe then I'll be able to find my own grain of sand. What do you think? . . . Yeah, I think it's time. ❖

Gómez refused to see the priest and yet, two days later his official burial takes place in a church in Maracay, bells tolling for his eternal rest. The newsperson, in a cracking voice, gives a long list of the medals that were placed on his coffin and the exact shape of his favorite horse's legs, the one that leads the funeral cortege. It's amazing how important people become when they die! Army, clergy, nuns, cabinet ministers, family members all walk toward the mausoleum while military planes salute. According to the epitaph, the dead man was a very good person. . . .

Knowing what the risks are, I go to the store to make sure everything is O.K. There is a strange quietness in every inch of every step I take. Several hours later the great silence explodes in the shouts of the people "El Bagre is dead, long live freedom!"

What follows is a nightmare. I'm not sure I can tell you about it because all of us, in our little cave, were very confused. Caracans gather in the Plaza Bolívar and carry placards demanding the death of all Gómez supporters, which is to say, the whole country! They destroy houses and furniture. They steal paintings and silverware. They burn cars. All this to the tune of

Por infeliz coincidencia
murieron el mismo día
el que liberó a Venezuela
y el que la tuvo fuñía . . .

By unhappy coincidence
the one who liberated Venezuela
and the one who screwed her
died on the same date. . . .

Luck or divine intervention? No one touches a single one of the musiús' stores. Nor of the big suppliers like Bensaya, Mauriente, or Zoriel. Thank goodness!

In any event, each one of us suffers stomachaches and palpitations. At home, these ailments were cured with a lot of tea, strawberry sauce, or apple pudding. Here we manage with cinnamon, maize blossom water, green plantain, and some herb brews prepared by Mrs. Gumer and which she also drinks in great big cups. "They're made of passionfruit, you know."

The chaos goes on for days. There are dead and wounded, and just as much anxiety as when the hordes would raze our villages. The mobs continue to destroy homes and villas, singing:

Gracias a Dios
Ya salimos
del yugo
donde nos tenía el verdugo. . . .

Thank god
we got rid of the yoke
in which the hangman held us.
. . . Long live freedom!
Long live Lopez Contreras.

That flat and dry voice is heard the next day on the radio making his first speech: "Our country is suffering a national misfortune because of the death of the leader who enriched the nation. . . ."

Could it really be the end of the world? We believe every word he says and don't show our faces on the streets. Now it's for real.

A day later, between spasms, Mrs. Gumer informs us that Eustoquio, the dictator's cousin and aspiring successor, was assassinated. He was shot right at the government offices on the corner of Gradillas and Monjas. The mob continued to torch cars of Gómez's cohorts demanding democratic elections.

"They say that in Eustoquio Gómez's burnt car thrown into the Guaire River there was over a million bolívares. And you know what else? His house on the corner of Marron and Cují was completely destroyed," she tells us.

The new president, thin and grey-skinned, begs for calm and wisdom. Gathered in our rooming house we have some wisdom but no calm. We await silently, what else can we do? No wonder they say "love your neighbor even if he plays the trumpet." When all is said and done, during those interminably long days, I can't help but remember how, when we arrived with one arm stretched out and the other behind our back, this place and these people took us in with open arms. Suitcase in hand, we walked freely through every twist and turn and road of their oppressed country, selling on time, on credit without any security or bondsman. No one ever bothered us. When we got here, all we asked for was to be allowed to carry our bundles on our shoulders, our moveable stores. And they let us.

It's also true that it was not all smooth as honey. On more than one night, the floor was our mattress and newspapers our blankets, because we had to take turns on the scarce number of beds, lice included. "Sleep quickly, we need the pillows!" Often things turned out terribly for me, but that was not the fault of the government or of the opposition.

"Do you think we should lock our meeting place?"

"No, why?"

"I don't know. I mean . . . look at the police, all around town, on foot and on horseback, followed by military trucks. It seems a state of siege."

"And what does that have to do with our brotherhood?"

"You're right. If they search us, what are they going to find? A first aid kit for emergencies with a few bolívares, just in case. And if they want us to translate our organizational charter, all the better, then they'll see how Gómez never wanted to grant us naturalization papers so we continue to be temporary residents."

"Thank god we didn't allow Venezuelan political issues in our sessions!"

"So what? I always thought it was strange not to have religion courses or plays or literary talks. Is that a sin? High treason or something?"

"Not to you, but to them, who knows? How could they understand that we have our own filtering process. That each of us must be over twenty-one and enjoy good reputation? They would die laughing if they found out that a person who steals, curses, or is syphilitic cannot join our group."

"Yeah, they would think we're some mysterious sect. Who knows what investigative methods they would use just out of curiosity to find out about us. So, shoo, relax and stay in . . . Lopez Contreras seems like a sensible person, let's hope."

How many times had Father told that story? Yet every time it sounded more amazing. A few days ago I saw a photocopy of the original letter . . . "Mr. President of the Republic . . . It's been four days since the *Köningsberg* arrived at the port of La Guaira and her Captain tells us it's impossible for him to stay any longer at port. Guided by our conscience and our humane obligation, and as we have been unable to find another solution to the plight of the one hundred and sixty refugees aboard, we appeal to your supreme authority and present this petition on their behalf. We hope that our prayers might find a favorable echo in your good Christian heart. The denial of this request on behalf of the refugees, which is their last resort, would result in their return to the German concentration camps with its obvious consequences."

It was a telegram dated March 3, 1939, addressed to López Contreras. The president's Christian heart was indeed moved. He granted them safe refuge. Max traveled to the dock as a member of the delegation in charge of taking care of these adopted immigrants. They were temporarily sheltered at Doctor Asa Sanchez's hacienda Mampote and from there, "dispersed throughout the land," as the government radio station spokesperson said.

A careful reading of the signatures shows that this was a high-caliber academic group. Of course they had to lie, after all Dr. Gabel, eminent German philosopher, was offering his services as a sausage maker, and Dr. Roilbert, a Polish woman with a doctorate in pharmacology, was offering her services as a corset maker and seamstress. The list went on. . . .

Three months later, the *Caribbea* arrived also without port of entry permit. Again the López government welcomed its condemned cargo. Nine years later, can you picture it? right there in the Miraflores Presidential House, Max the musiú was the interpreter of the dialogue between a foreign Jewish delegate and President Rómulo Gallegos:

"Mr. President, why do your foreign consulates state that they do not grant visas to blacks, Chinese, or Jews?"

"That law precedes my presidency and I believe we should abolish it. The fact is, people of all colors and creeds can come to this country. And I'm glad to say that you certainly are proof of that."

Being at the seat of power scared the Jew from Lendov: "Oy, was I petrified! The president was very tall and serious and had a thunderous voice. Here there was absolute freedom, and Gallegos was a very fine human being, but the fear of the Gómez dictatorship didn't vanish over night! The criollo and tender-hearted doctor is a real *mensch*, warm and generous with the foreigners he calls endearingly *musiú*, a word derived from the French *monsieur*.

"Yet I feel sometimes that all the unresolved problems of this inefficient and corrupt democracy could, in a moment of deep crisis, explode in national chauvinism. Sound like a newspaper editorial, Doctor? Or just paranoia? What do you think?" ❖

There was national paralysis. Nobody worked. What could I do? We musiús aren't factory workers or government employees. We certainly are not military personnel ready for war, unemployed, beggars, political militants, or even union members in fact. Once again, just like in Poland, we were on the sidelines of everything and in the middle of nothing. . . .

True, in Valencia we did organize a committee of peddlers. We needed licenses according to a new law the governor of Carabobo enacted just before I left for Caracas. Guess who was the president? Anyway, I only accepted the job because it was supposed to be like a free trade union. No Communism. No ties. It's no coincidence that the table at which we sat was round! In fact I'm president in name only, because all of us, Rosenberg, Shnaiderman, Konefka, Vilner, Waisenberg, Topel, Sonenshein, Landau—we all share responsibilities. Why? Because everyone has to do whatever is needed. A community like this is too heavy a load for one person, and believe me, zero politics. When we arrived, nobody promised us even one little crumb and we certainly have no right to demand it. Anyway, one lie is a lie, two are lies, but three lies turn into politics. Did you know that? I learned that in our secret meetings in Lendov and later in Cuba. However, Gómez's death did open up new horizons for the country's development. It's impressive how happy the people are to tear down the La Rotunda jail and throw all the chains into the ocean. This is what I wrote, in March, in the *Forward,* the newspaper that saved my life before, in Tampa, remember? Since it is completely written in Yiddish, no Gentile reads it, but our brothers all over the world do.

Part of me becomes used to writing a monthly page for the paper. It's as if the tyrant's death had liberated me, in those uncertain days, to appoint myself unpaid spokesperson of our very frightened little group.

I wrote home a lot too. "Dear Parents, thank god and with his help things are going well for me," and I always included my articles. I wanted them to be proud of my new role as our chronicler.

A teacher without a classroom? Journalism might just be the magic solution.

She was finally free to divulge hidden agendas and, to everyone, since a newspaper column is like a classroom without walls, with thousands of listeners. Of course she misses looking into their eyes, the voice nuances, the arguments, and their participation. But she senses these, and directs her words to each and everyone.

Oh, her very own name in bold letters! An old passion, rekindled and automatically reactivated by that puffed up ego of hers. "You're an amazing reporter!" "You write with your ovaries!" "There's no end to your daring!" Followed by the expected: "Your excellency the Minister requests the pleasure of your company. . . ." "The President invites you to . . ." "The Minister of Culture would appreciate your presence at . . ."

Ah, the delirium of fame! Me, me, and more me! Almost like power! Almost. "Thank you very much, Ladies and Gentlemen. But . . . I write because I don't know how to do anything else. At least not right now, and I have no other aspirations. . . . Half a century ago, a bunch of musiús began arriving. They knocked on doors in order to sell rags. They knocked: clap, clap, clap. Or as we would say: knock, knock. They chose the word *cláper,* one who claps, to define themselves. So, daughter of a cláper, I too am a caller. When I knock and knock from the press room, what I wish to sell for free is what we might call ethical anxiety, because only under such a state of mind can one analyze one's own mental vices. . . . I feel that the country today is like the cartoon figure of Don Fulgencio, the eternal child/adult because he lacked a childhood. It suffers from a lack of a very precious and fundamental element needed to grow up with maturity. What is it, you ask? The ambition to realize oneself in a job that one likes and its immediate derivative, the satisfaction of achievement. . . . Can you understand that?"

"Wow, professor! You speak so well!" "You'd be a great consultant to the Board of Education!" "Would you agree to run as an independent within our party?" "We need thinkers in our think tank, join us and a chauffeur will always be at your disposal."

No thank you! She'd be a horrible professional politician. Lacks talent, patience, and the ability to plot intrigues. Furthermore, she dislikes direct contact with groups who decide, by totalitarian majority, the squareness of a circle. . . .

"My dearest parents, and brothers and sisters, I am fine. Please don't worry about me. I'm working very hard and have my own small business. Together with these words I send a few dollars, only a little, because I'm saving the rest to give you in person. I'm also including some articles I wrote for the *Forward*."

Gottenyu, what pleasure I got out of putting together those words every month! Sure, business might make you a king, but it robs you of tranquility and takes you away from all pleasant pastimes. It is so hard to split yourself. Like trying to mix oil and water. Buying and selling and reading and thinking and writing. I guess that's what they mean when they say that he who studies has no head for business. Also, I never stop doing my community work. I collect money so that our charitable society can provide for those in need. . . . Don't ask me where I find the time. . . . But, my Poppinyu used to say: "Always remember that we fall by ourselves, but we need a friendly hand to help us get up."

Generous and giving Rifka helped solve Father's problem by harmonizing household and business chores. She managed the business while at the same time keeping tight, if remote, control over the family and the house. It was, in fact, because of her tight supervision that the girls studied hard and a little was put away for a modest dowry. . . .

Max gave himself completely to others. Like the cláper he was, he walked and knocked on doors for days, months, and years in order to buy Turkish lands in Palestine, build the new Community Social Center, create and build a community school, erect a new first aid center and a cultural center for Yiddish speakers:

"I've got to get housing for Shloime who's getting on in years and has no one to care for him, but wants to spend his last days at the Wailing Wall. And what about the widow Yente Lustiker, an invalid, and poor Fishale, who went broke? *US*, the literary magazine, needs funds, and what about Herzog the writer whose work focuses on the Hasidic themes in Martin Buber's works. . . ."

He never sought homage, nor did we ever see him at the dining room table presiding over issues involving "important" members of our comumunity. His name was never printed in bronze letters nor on little plaques anywhere. No rewards, no certificates, no diplomas. He never sought them and they were never offered. . . . ❖

Help our neighbors? Yes, one must always help. Nu? so if that's true, I should begin with my very own and go home to see for myself what's going on. In Gardel's song he says:

Ya adivino el parpadeo
De las luces que a lo lejos
Van marcando mi retorno . . .
Volver. . . .

I can make out the flickering lights
That from afar
guide my return
Return . . .
Volver. . . .

Yes, I need the scent of family. . . .

This of course means I've got to close "Bargain Corner." Well, let me tell you, it's much easier to start a business than to get rid of one. This is one of my American discoveries. Another and more hurtful one is that a man cannot be called a real man until he is joined to a woman he loves. And the third revelation which will haunt me to the day I die is that we are about to enter the dark cave of this infamous century. Do I have to spell out the name of that tumor or is it enough for me to say: Hitler, Mussolini, and Franco?

You see, after Gómez's death, the press was free. The news wires began to tell us of the turbulent cloud that was enveloping a world blind because it chose not to see. Truth is so heavy only a few dare carry it. When you add to this the fact that fifteen million unemployed Americans are voting for a second term for the polio-ridden Roosevelt plus the fact that in dear old Mother Russia, Stalin keeps inventing ways of getting rid of anyone who doesn't see things his way, you get a pretty good picture of what the world looked like.

Right then and there, three of the poet Iankev Glatshtein's verses turned into real poetry for me:

Good night
Wide and foul world
I, not you, choose to slam the door. . . .

To top it all off, after being here for six years, I finally discover the real Venezuela! Most of her three and a half million people can't read or write! Bless you a thousand times, Luis José Hernandez, wherever you might be! You who gave me hours and hours of your time that first week here while we were both under the roof of that kind American gentleman. You taught me to read and pronounce the Spanish alphabet. Me no less. Me, a nobody from Lendov who spoke Polish without knowing its letters! To me you were every bit as wise and great as my childhood teacher of Sacred Texts. Did I follow all your good advice? No. I didn't always read the newspapers. After all, I had to earn my daily *arepa*-bread, you know how it is. But now, when the truth about your country is becoming known, I remember you! . . . Where are you? "He just disappeared, we don't know where to," said the new maid at the American's house when I went to visit you. Were you, I wonder, one of the many forced to swallow broken glass at the Rotunda? Or one of those who was slowly extinguished at Puerto Cabello's death house? Who will ever know? . . .

The newspapers say that we foreigners make up 2 percent of the population. A little island in a sick ocean where eight out of every ten gentlemen has blennorrhea and one in ten syphilis. That's not counting malaria, typhus, tuberculosis, and the worst disease of all, poverty. Life expectancy is thirty-four years. Can you believe that? I'm just about to become a statistic in my new country. . . .

So, you might ask, why do I stay? Is it only because the people are kind and can laugh at their own pain? Is it because earning a living and saving money is that easy to do? And where would it be better? But gottenyu, not even in Lendov, in those rare peaceful times, did a hundred and thirty out of a thousand children die before their first birthday! . . . Oy yoy yoy, only the massacring hordes can beat that macabre record.

You want to know the truth? Well, I'll tell you. This is the only place on earth where a good-for-nothing like me, without a trade, can earn a living and not be bothered.

What's the big deal about writing under the pressure of censorship? Who cares anyway? Do you really think that all your words, when they're actually printed, are of any use to anyone? Have you managed to change anything? Why don't you just admit it, you're a useless failure.

For two whole weeks she kept calling the editor of the newspaper, but his very competent secretary carried out her duties so well that he was shielded from her anger. She wanted to hear from his very own lips why he vetoed the publication of her article on Werner von Braun, Hitler's famous engineer, creator of the V-2 missile which the Nazis shot over London in 1949. The eminent scientist had come to Venezuela an American citizen with a clean past and great fame. He had, after all, led the NASA group that launched America's first satellite into orbit in 1959 and the Saturn rocket that took the first man to the moon.

"Thank you for seeing me, Sir."

"What's the reason for your insistence?"

"Hunt is more like it, wouldn't you say? Well, I demand to know why you censored my piece on von Braun."

"He was a guest of our government."

"I know that, but is this newspaper a government mouthpiece?"

"No, of course not, but it would have been a slap in the face. . . ."

"Excuse me, Sir? I don't seem to understand . . ."

"We considered your point of view rather unfortunate. . . ."

"You mean, Sir, telling the world what von Braun did during the Third Reich is unfortunate? It's a historical fact! One of many that our young people are totally ignorant about. And anyway, that focus or point of view, as you call it, was mine and not the newspaper's."

"The editor, by virtue of his position, has the right to make those decisions."

"Yes, of course, I understand. . . . Good night, Sir."

Here in the bosom of a democracy, thirty some odd years after Treblinka and Guernica, she came to understand that the von Brauns of this world would never have succeeded without the support of these "Sirs," that fascism is not a fad or an ism but a timeless and amoral way of being.

She gave up journalism in that milieu of liberals where she met with no support for her complaints and she came back to it four years later when that "Sir editor" concluded his reign. Writing and silence were synonymous around here . . . she was dispensable. . . . ❖

The voice of the people like god's—blessed be his name—can't be silenced. And I'm scared. Because when people are given freedom and power, after a long tyranny, they're worse than the despot was. After thirty years, this boiling pot spills and spreads vengeance. Let me tell you. Some call it the exercise of free democracy. As far as I'm concerned, worrying about politics is hell. If you know how to abuse your smile, you are ready for public office and further away from heaven.

Speaking of boiling pots of oil, there is one on the burner right near our club. Students can be seen going in and out at all hours of the day and night. I keep going by just to make sure our meeting house is O.K. Something is going on in there for sure. Two seem to get more attention than the others. One is a nervous blond whom they call Jóvito and others refer to as the "man from Miracielos Street." The other, whose name is Rómulo, is shorter, more reserved, and wears glasses, just like an intellectual.

My landlady warns us: "Keep your eyes open, my dear musiús. There are presidential spies everywhere. I hear that each and every one of those who gather in that house at the corner is an honest-to-goodness Commie! They'll all be caught sooner or later, mark my words. . . . Be very careful not to be seen in a group or they'll think you guys are also freemasons and stuff like that. Above all, don't let those beards of yours be seen and for goodness sake don't do anything stupid. All I need is to have them shut down my rooming house because of you!"

We closed the club for a few weeks and decided not to be anywhere near it. We don't go to our stores or business either because day in and day out, there is some sort of meeting or other, at Plaza Bolívar or the New Circus, or any corner for that matter, where up to two thousand people show up. The demonstrations against President López are disbanded with the help of machetes and guns. I'm not worried about the loss of money; after all, the poor man is not the one who has little but rather the one who reaches too high. What does drive me insane is to be locked up in my room, just like in Lendov when we suspected a pogrom. Here it's the government who forces you to stay in. Since that very large gathering at the Bolívar Park, where four were killed and over a hundred wounded, López suspended all constitutional rights and declared a curfew from five in the afternoon. If they catch you talking to one or two people, on any street, you'll be arrested without questions. Do you see what I'm saying?

The same night of the problems at the plaza, in mid February, they called for a workers' strike. Seventy, eighty thousand Caracans? I don't know, I'd never seen so many people gathered. It was scary. They walk toward the university building, you know the pretty one, behind the capitol which from the outside looks so much like the one in Havana. From there they proceed to Miraflores, the seat of government, with banners demanding "Down with the Gómez party!" "Freedom of speech for the Trade Unions!" "Reinstate Civil Rights!" "Down with censorship!"

The volcano erupted into liberal, anti-Communist, popular, nationalist, unitarian, and who knows how many other political parties. Someone named Machado declared: "I'm a Communist!" So our compatriot Motek Leivik gets hold of a copy of the Red Book and under cover of darkness at the Municipal Theater, we search to see if any of us appears in the book as a Soviet sympathizer. Who among us doesn't feel a little guilty about this clandestine operation? Who among us didn't flirt with Bolshevik ideas as a youngster back home? None of ours appear on the list. Thank you, gottenyu. It would have been a death sentence for sure, even if only one had appeared, we would have all . . .

Vincent Gerbasi's poetry was very much hers, and she had in fact often wondered . . .

> *Venimos de la noche y hacia la noche vamos*
> *Los pasos en el polvo, el fuego de la sangre,*
> *el sudor de la frente, la mano sobre el hombro,*
> *el llanto en la memoria,*
> *todo queda cerrado por anillos de sombra. . . .*
>
> *We came from darkness and towards darkness we go*
> *Footsteps in the sand, fire in the blood*
> *the sweat of our brow, hand on shoulder*
> *tears in our memory*
> *all is locked into circles of shadows. . . .*

She had also always wondered about that uncomfortable "chosen people" epithet. She came to know that for ten centuries, during the Middle Ages, it was used to personify the guilt of a deicide and that during Napoleon's liberalism, the Monarchists used it to designate a fearful Masonic sect. To the tzar's right wingers, to Henry Ford and Adolf Hitler these "chosen people" were "Communist perverts," and according to Father Stalin they had to be eliminated because of their complicity with Yankee imperialism. Ahhhh yes, "chosen" to fuel the bonfires, gas chambers, purges, battles and terrorists' bombs.

It wasn't hard to figure out the purpose of this illustrious and hardly divine chosenness. . . . She had always suspected that "we come from darkness. . . ."

Holy Week is here. On Wednesday the stores are still open. From the minute I leave my boarding house I notice men and women of all ages and in large numbers wearing dark purple tunics made of heavy cloth. Some are kneeling as if they were really crippled.

I decide to follow that strange silent parade and arrive at the Basílica of Sta. Teresa packed with parishioners. That afternoon, after closing,

I go by again and at that time, I see from afar a wooden Jesus, dragging himself under the weight of an enormous crucifix. They refer to him as the Nazarene of St. Paul. He proceeds very slowly at the center of the crowd that accompanies him all around the church neighborhood. As he goes by, people cross themselves and beg his help for their many sorrows.

That immense crucifix becomes my martyrdom. No one has pointed me out as a criminal, but, once again I can feel the hatred I felt back in Lendov, when the Christian procession for Holy Week would always end in stonings, beatings, and bloodshed. . . .

Como un asesino que acecha
puñal en mano
a su víctima
en altas horas de la noche
así acecho tus pases, díos mío.
Mira, tu piedad
nunca me ha sonreído todavía a mí
el nieto de Iscariot . . .

Like an assassin who lurks
knife in hand
waiting for his victim
in the early hours of the morning
so I search out your steps my god
your mercy has not yet smiled upon me
I the grandson of Judas Iscariot. . . .

Once again, the answer comes from the poet Itzik Manger whose verses I read so often yet only now have become truly mine. Thank you, Itzik!

I run to bathe and dress because that same night we celebrate our first night Passover Seder. Nu? After all, wasn't the other one, the so-called Last Supper, a paschal meal too?

We gather in the modern house of the very religious Tolders. From the United States they got kosher wine and the bread of affliction, matzoh to remind us of the manna our ancestors ate during the forty-year journey through the desert on the way to the Holy Land of Abraham, Isaac, and Jacob.

As if in unison, the whole group chants,

> *"We were the Pharaoh's slaves in Egypt from where He took us with a firm hand and an outstretched arm."*

Then one true voice, the Berger's youngest son, asks the four questions that answer:

> *"Why is this night different from any other night?"*

We partake of bitter herbs because our forced captivity by the Egyptians was bitter; we eat hard-boiled eggs dipped in salted water in order to reproduce life submerged in the tears of slavery. You know something though? To me, eggs dipped in salted water comes from the fact that I always thought our brothers got them wet when they crossed the Red Sea. God knows I mean no disrespect with this theory, but the way I see it, he wouldn't have made things that easy for us by just separating the waters so that we could flee. To me that makes no sense at all. What would that do to our fighting spirit? No. I think Moses was a pretty smart fellow and he crossed at the narrowest point during dry season, just like I did, when I crossed the Oder and I'm not even half as tall as Moses was. No. He, like me, took advantage of the low tide. The others probably died. So, nu? Where is the miracle, you ask? Ah, in that Moses calculated right! He saved enough of us so that we could continue to exist as a people. Believe me, that's a miracle!

We also had some chopped apples mixed with wine and nuts to remind ourselves of the mortar with which, year after year, we cemented together the gigantic bricks used to build the pyramids you admire so much today and which have lasted for centuries. Weren't we, after all, the cheapest labor around?

At the end of that same week, I witness a grotesque scene. On several street corners they burn a rag doll named Judas. It's a puppet, dressed like us, in white linen suits and ties. Before setting him on fire, they hang him. I pretend not to understand but the mocking hurts just the same. I know that once again a fellow Jew is paying for a thousand-year-old sin, only this one is made of cloth and straw. To the mob's great delight, it turns into ashes.

I thank you, gottenyu, that this time, today, here, now, I'm not the flesh and blood victim. . . .

On that hot June day in 1967, the Middle East was an infernal fire. She went to teach and took the little transistor radio with her in her purse to catch the news whenever possible. Tulio Rensendo García Yánez, gaunt and polite and chair of the History Department, sat next to her on a bench.

"Well, well, my dear colleague. You seem a bit upset. Tell me something: if war were to break out between Venezuela and the State of Israel, what side would you take?"

"Well, if there were ever war declared between Cuba and Venezuela, in which army would you serve?'"

"That's not the issue."

"My answer nevertheless is the same. Did you put the question to Bruna Greci who is Italian, or María de los Angeles González who is very much Spanish, or to Manuel Oliveira Dos Santos, the corner store owner who is most certainly Portuguese?"

"You people are different."

"Yes, of course, I forgot. So your question really is: how come you people always have double loyalties?"

"Yeah, something like that."

"Well, I guess I'm just part of this weak and imperfect human race, unlike a robot, and because of that I seem to hang on to multiple loyalties. I love so many people and things at the same time. . . . I think that everyone should fight for this privilege, you know, this privilege which is true democracy. So far as I know, the Fascists, both of the left and the right, are the only ones who have an exclusive nationalistic loyalty."

García turned white. He tried to leave, but she grabbed him violently.

"Just a second please, listen to me, Tulio. . . ."

"Well, evidently you misunderstood what . . ."

"On the contrary, I understood perfectly. In fact, let me put it in context. Our left, the one that calls itself revisionist and new, is simply repeating an ancient accusation, only now it has a new name. I'm guilty of life, because my cousin Salim Ben-Mussad doesn't have his own lands. I took them from him. Now as then. After all, let's face it, I am the great-great-great-granddaughter of a traitor who, according to the Church Fathers, sold god for a few coins."

"Now, my dear Professor, you must admit that that is historically accurate."

"You know that official story by heart, don't you? But do you ever really know with a Venezuelan of Arab descent what his position is on OPEC's internal power struggles? Let me tell you, that's the kind of question you really should be asking yourself, because it's loaded with a heavy dose of patriotism."

Shaken, she went home early. An exquisite stained-glass window, lovingly painted for almost thirty years, began to crack. . . .

Here between us, Dad, excuse me, I mean Doctor, García Yánez had a point. Country is . . . well, family, exchanging gifts in December, Jerusalem the Eternal, Paul Newman, the colonial house of my childhood in San José, Mount Avila, Haifa at night, Siboney, Alma Llanera, Polonaises and Mazurkas, Duke Ellington, Tevye the dairyman who fiddles on the roof. . . . Country is . . . my soul in pain. . . . I'm a whore. . . . ❖

After the Easter festivities, I read in the newspaper *Religion,* or was it the *Herald,* that a small group of rebellious students was demanding the expulsion of the Jesuits and other religious orders. . . . Funny how a toothache makes you forget a migraine. . . . My heart is heavy. Then, on the radio, I hear a young man, a Catholic by the name of Caldera, denouncing this as an assault against freedom. I applaud him in silence. My spirit returns to my body. This time I'm on the priest's side. Their black *soutaines* look like sun-filled tunics. What would my sweet David of Lendov, may he rest in peace, say if he knew?

Oy yoy yoy. The thermometer keeps rising while the blood of our veins freezes with fear. President López , without much calm but with great prudence, addresses the nation almost daily. I listen on Radio Caracas, which is the new name of Broadcasting.

The president was extremely bony and his skinny neck looked like a giraffe's. That's why my roommates used to say that "Sport Fix" was about to speak on the radio. "Sport Fix" was the fashionable shirt label whose slogan was: "Your neck speaks for you. . . ."

López is displeased. He warns that the Caracas agitators waste strength and time inciting riots and vagrancy while in the interior of the country, thousands of workers work hard to feed the citizenry, including the rabble rousers themselves. . . . That's what he says, more or less. . . .

"Uy, yuy, yuy. 'El Ronquito' is sure angry now—may God find us confessed and pure!"

"Tell me, Mr. Pancho. Do you think it would be safer to go back to selling from door to door in Valencia, like I used to?"

Don Francisco Pomenta, ex-prisoner of the illustrious patriot López, specializing in anti-Gómez activity, and my new housemate, meditates and laughs. "Why don't all you Syrian peddlers go and work in the Callao mines, over there in the jungles of Guayana where there is tons and tons of gold all over the place instead of staying here, worrying about every little thing?"

"We didn't come to steal hidden treasures, let alone be food for snakes, Mr. Pancho. We want to earn our bread with hard work and sweat. Not with deceit."

"Well, then, you're pretty stupid because with this dictatorship pretending to be a democracy, you're neither here nor there."

"What do you mean?"

"Sure. Look. López is a weak son of a bitch. Since there is no more torture allowed, any creature called a Communist gets thrown in a cat's sack and zap! shipped abroad and left to manage as best he can."

"And tell me, don Pancho, why did they call Gómez catfish?"

"Hell, because it's a river fish that feeds on excrement! You know, 'catfish' himself asked the question of one of his associates and they say that when he heard the answer he said: 'Aha, well then get away from me or I'll eat you!' And you know what, he did. He ate us all, even the ones who were not dung, just in case. Don't I know it!"

Francisco is really something else. Roughened by blows and full of scars and charm, one day he asks me, puzzled: "What happened to 'four eyes?'"

"Who?"

"You know, your friend, the one with glasses, did he go back to Syria?"

"Oh, you mean Iglaiski? Has a bad cough and they send him to Los Teques to breathe pure air. . . ."

I take advantage of his question to ask something I always wanted to know:

"Why do people around here always use different words when they speak? Is it because they've always been afraid of the government and must say everything in code? I had a customer, Hortensia Montiel, who almost gave me a heart attack at her door in the El Valle area.

She yells: 'Look out for the bull, alligator!' And so I turn around, thinking that the beasts are at my feet, and guess what? Not even a fly! Then she tells me she has no money, which of course I understand by her gestures. 'Musiú, I'm broke. Take your music somewhere else. Maybe next Sunday, we'll see. Anyway, I just owe you four garlic peels.' Another, Lourdes Padrón, who lives in Santa Rosalía where she works as a maid, yells through the shutter of the carriage entrance: 'Ay ay, the fruit man is on my back!' 'I assure you young lady,' I say, 'that I never sold you any fruit whatsoever. All I sold you were floral fabrics, that's what it says right here on the card, see?' 'Ah, and on top of everything you're pulling my leg too?' 'Anyway, when will you pay?' 'When the frog grows hair!'"

Francisco listens attentively, so I go on. "You know something, Pancho? One has to be a language expert in order to translate this type of speech. . . ."

"No, my friend, one just has to be a wise ass." He laughs out loud and then suddenly stops. "If it weren't for these pleasant moments and those of hunger. . . ."

His face changes again. His somber face lights up and he looks at me: "Hey, want to listen to your idol's last tango, written just before he died? Well, go get your guitar. Here goes, for your collection:

Ya adivino el brujuleo
de los Gómez que a lo lejos
van tramando su retorno.
Son los mismos que arrancaron
con sus ávidos manejos
el dinero y la nación. . . .

I can guess the witchcraft
of the Gómezes who from afar
plot their return.
They're the same ones who greedily took

the people's money.
And though they may not want me to
I'll return
Because one always returns to one's first love
The quiet valleys where the Catfish said,
"This is my *cattle,*
my *sugar cane."*

After the last chord of my guitar I smile and Francisco asks ironically: "Gardel was pretty sentimental, don't you think?"

"Yes, yes. . . ."

I remember that conversation very well; it was the longest one I ever had with Pancho. It was on a national holiday in fact. Shortly after that, he went out one morning and no one ever heard from him again. No one even asked. You know what I mean?

But that afternoon, after a lot of joking around, he suddenly became very serious: "How about becoming my son's godfather, next Sunday in Turmero? There'll be a great stew!"

"What's this all about?"

"You know, to be the godfather at the baptism. The priest sprinkles some Holy Water on the baby's head while you hold him in your arms."

"Heavens, what an honor, Mr.Pancho! Unfortunately I'm afraid my religion doesn't allow me to participate in this rite."

"And what's your religion, anyway?"

"Listen, someone once asked the same of my father. I heard when he said that an ancient wise man answered in one sentence: 'What is hateful to you, never do to your neighbor.' That's the whole law, everything else is commentary."

"But wait a minute, that's from the Ten Catholic, Apostolic, and Roman Commandments! So, would you be angry if I were to be godfather to a son of yours?"

"I'm not in the least offended, but neither do I ask it of you."

"What's your name again?"

"It's Freilich, that means 'happy.'"

"Wrong name for you! Your name should be 'sorrow' because you're always so melancholic and tearful. . . ."

I'm sure Pancho never understood why Hillel's little sentence forbade us from being related this way. And to be honest with you, neither did I. I did, however, go to Turmero as a guest. I took a good gift. "Use it in good health," I said and then was witness to a fantasy. At the church and at the reception, Pancho Pomenta's three wives and ten children all gathered, just like in an Arab's harem. Together they celebrated the baptism and confirmation with a party that lasted all day. At first I really enjoyed the music of the group led by Margarito Suarez. There was a violin, flute, banjo, cornet, and a harp, just like King Saul's, maybe even bigger! The little orchestra reminds me of our little orchestra in Lendov. It sounds very good . . . .

I taste some of the food. A little bit of stew. A little bit of figs in syrup. Two little bites of something they call *torta burrera* ("donkey's cake") and tiny little bananas that are a wonderful delicacy. But then, things turn sour. Pancho notices that I am a little sad so, to cheer me up he says: "Take a little drink! Just one won't make you a drunkard!" To be polite I drink a little of something mixed with wine they call *sangría*. You know what? That deceitful alcohol, which seemed such an innocent drink, added to the stifling heat of the place which, like Artemisa in Cuba, seems to be built above the fire; anyway, the whole thing knocked me out, right then and there and in front of everybody. I woke up in a stranger's house. Oy vey, was I ever embarrassed. I said I was sick to my stomach (which was true!) and fled on the 4:00 bus back to Caracas.

She had made it a rule never to go to any cocktail parties, official or private, honoring the "New Venezuela of the seventies." She decided to make an exception in this case because the entire Venezuelan intelligentsia would be gathered at this glamorous event and she needed more signatures for her protest against the Soviet Union's oppression of minorities, and the release of jailed dissidents.

The majestic hall of the hotel is haughtily illuminated and the multiplicity of floral arrangements reflected into infinity by the extraordinary mirrors. Some fifty waiters impeccably attired in black and white dance around like penguins among the five hundred guests. A small handful of them behind the lilac-colored canopy were in charge of the hors d'oeuvres and Dom Perignon, Brut and Cuvée Special, imported by the government especially for this event and served in fluted glasses, of course. The continuous sounds of corks popping reminded her of firecrackers. As it's a bit warm, the bottles of Old Parr, Ancestor, and Chivas Regal whiskey are kept open and consumed on the rocks, straight and with soda, as fashion demands.

Platters of *saumon fumé* surrounded by the blackest of pumpernickel and caviar urns, overflowing with Iranian Beluga sprinkled with vodka, are devoured. Next come Chinese delicacies: sweet and sour ribs, chicken dumplings and shrimp balls. Miniature quiches, and lobster tarts with mushrooms add the indispensable French touch. And, let's not forget the quail eggs, roast beef, and pigs-in-a-blanket.

Occasionally, a bluish smoke and a distinctly unpleasant odor disturb the sensibilities of the guests. Common people frying and consuming greasy *tequeños* on a nearby street. The gentlemen all standing stiffly reminded her of the cod liver oil man on the Scott's Emulsion she was forced to take as a kid to try to "put some meat" on her bones. The ladies all standing on one leg, like storks, elegantly and tastefully shift from one to the other at discreet intervals. Everyone's hands are impressively occupied. Some holding cigarettes, others glasses, and napkins. If there should happen to be a free hand, it is assigned the job of holding a fashionable satin purse or a silky evening bag.

Who, how, and why would anyone here want to sign the petition she now carefully hides from view? She runs away. The petition untouched and hidden in her big sloppy leather shoulder bag . . . They were celebrating the publication of Flor de Icaco, a book of poems by Victor Ledezma Berrieitía, congressman from the State of Cojedes. She ran away, stunned, nauseous, dizzy. . . .

Wouldn't you call that phobic behavior, Doctor? ❖

After a few months the violence stopped. President López Contreras shipped the opposition out, saying that too many captains sink a ship. Now that the streets are quiet, I can handle my exile a little better, but I'm anguished over what's happening in Europe, just like a deaf man imagines what he can't hear. . . .

The following year was very profitable. The number of customers doubled, my profits grew, and I saved every penny of it. I knew I had to go back home, and who knows, I thought maybe I'd stay and open a little shop in Lendov.

One fatal day I receive the news I'd been dreading and thinking about in countless sleepless nights: Poppa and Momma dead within five months of each other, Oy gottenyu! Then and there I put the store up for sale, I practically give it away. My nerves explode as I come to realize that just as splinters between stones is a natural way to make a joint, so greed is the natural element between buyer and seller. . . . Anyway, finally I lock up and hand over the place.

Good-bye Caracas. I leave an orphan. We are all children until we lose our parents. Is there any other way to describe the sense of abandonment of an orphan? Oy yoy yoy, with no father or mother, you're a defenseless old man, no matter how old you are.

I do run into some luck, however. Two new friends help me through my misery. Aaron Brand, a freckled Rumanian from Nova Zulitza, says he's planning to go back very soon. He had been in San Salvador and Perú, but things just didn't work out. God, how I love to listen to him. He's so learned in Scripture and like me, a lover of verse. The other one, Isidore Sponki, cultured and very modest, speaks in a low hum. He is an upholsterer who reads Dostoevski, Marx, and all our writers as if he were a librarian. He left Sokolov and spent time in Bogotá before coming here. Like Nathaniel, who married Talia two weeks ago, he came the year of the Wall Street crash, when Colombian coffee wasn't worth a penny. . . . He buys a home for his wife and three children in the working-class neighborhood of Sarria where he opens a hardware store selling punch bowls, jars, pewter chamber pots. He reads and reads, humming Italian opera and country ballads.

The night before I leave the three of us go to the Ritz Soda Fountain, the one on the corner of Principal and Monjas. They cry silently as they give me envelopes for Poland and Rumania. No one says "see you soon" or even "good-bye."

The next morning, very early, they show up at my rooming house. They close their business to take me to the boat, can you believe that? I remembered the tango:

Adiós muchachos
compañe-ros de mi vi-da
me toca a mi hoy emprender la retirada. . . .

Good-bye
my life-long companions
today it is my turn to leave. . . .

Red noses, wet handkerchiefs, mumblings in Yiddish: "Don't forget to send our letters through the French mail." "Let us know immediately what's going on at home!"

"Don't worry, my brothers. I'll write very soon. Shalom! Peace be with you!"

She will make a supreme effort to adapt once again to the neighborhood of her adolescence. It may not even be so unconscious, actually, her decision to rent an apartment in the old neighborhood of

San Leopoldino now that she's a grown woman. She's given herself a dare because her father always says "it's easy to love humanity, but hard to love one person!" With great relish, she broadcasts publicly her right to be herself and the right of any minority to its full realization. But she still carries deep within her some of Portnoy's Complaint: a resistance to being completely where it smells like gefilte fish, where you hear village gossip and constant *kvetching*.

In the same building, there're some war survivors from New Zulitza, where her partner is also from. Amazing how a town of three streets somehow managed to populate half the globe!

"How is it possible that being from the same place and now neighbors, and thirty years ago from the very same block, you can treat them so coldly?" That's the daily complaint. She had to be who and what she was and to accept them for what they were, without makeup and without concessions to either balcony or orchestra. Otherwise, she was and would always be a false activist, and not a true fighter for human rights. ❖

The Horacio was a maddening turtle. This time I travel first class, but am more uncomfortable and lonely than on my previous journey, when I was among the poor in third class. The books that Brand and Sponki lent me as well as the newspapers I took from our social club are my faithful travel companions. I really enjoy reading this paper because each page is like a pocket dictionary. You can find whatever you want in it. There's poetry, world politics, health books, antique books, new books galore, and always humour, the good kind, you know what I mean?

At Le Havre, where I saw the ocean ten years ago for the first time, I am met by David Haftarchik, an old friend from Lendov who's been married for about seven months to a Polish redhead. They met at the cooperative leather workshop where they are both cutters and sewers. I'm warmly received in his tiny, bathroom-less apartment.

While I wait for a Polish visa, hard to come by since I am now a naturalized Venezuelan citizen, I take in this beautiful city. It is a lot noisier now with all the car traffic, but you can still hear the singing of the sparrows and feel as though you were at an open air concert.

In the bright sunlight, or by lighted street lamps, I walk around the Champs Elysées. I am delighted by the historical street names and avenues: George the Fifth, Danton, Jacob, Balzac. Also, at almost all the outdoor cafes and Metro stations they're collecting money for the Spanish Republicans. Twenty days in beautiful Paris, going from one end to the other while my hosts work. David brings me our newspapers: *Kadima, Parisier Haint,* and *Naie Presse,* all very up to date. . . . They confirm my deepest fears over the black cloud which spreads from the steppes of Jose Chugasvili throughout the continent, over the Third Reich and all the way here. I got to see the International Exposition just barely before it closed and of all the exhibits, beautifully displayed, which do you think was the most visible? The German one, of course! Its gigantic flag with the swastika could be clearly seen from all angles of the fair and even from several angles of the city itself! Oy yoy yoy, may Joseph and Adolph only turn into lamps, that hang all day, and burn all night!

Helen, Haftarchik's wife, is from Kalisz and hasn't seen her family for six years. She cries often when she thinks of them and it makes her husband suffer: "She's afraid to go visit, because the attacks against us get more intense with each passing day, but, if she could go with you? I leave her in your hands. Take care of her and of yourself! God bless . . . !"

And so, with very heavy hearts, we leave for Poland. At the German border, from Poznan on, I feel a horrible foreboding. And at five that morning when we get to the Kalisz station, not a soul there to greet us! How come nobody came to meet us? Did the telegram get lost? Did something happen?

In two hours no chauffeur wants to take us to the Moses neighborhood where the Brockman family is waiting for us. Now we see very clearly why nobody came to pick us up. Finally, a little after seven, a very special cart goes by. I guess that the "driver" is one of us because he's on foot and doing the horse's job. The reins that pull the cart are tied to his shoulders. Gottenyu, he's is still a boy, but already all bent and in shredded rags. . . . He smiles, toothless. . . . Happy to earn a few cents taking the luggage to our area of town.

At last I manage to hail a Polish taxi. Unwillingly but for double the price, the driver will take us to the suburb of the "other." Oh, yes, Poland is ruled by a Constitution and everyone is a citizen, except the Yankelovichs, the Bernsteins, and the Goldbergs. Sure everyone has equal rights, but they can't exercise them because of:

"Who's to blame for this disaster?"

"We and the cyclists."

"But, why the cyclists?"

"Nu, why us?"

But wait, because Kalisz is just the first stage of the apocalypse, seen in slow motion. It isn't even my kind of movie. Veis meir, how I wish someone would wake me from this nightmare. If only it were just a film.

Helen's family, the very kind Brockmans, treat me like the King of Persia for the time I'm there. And since I'm a marriageable American, they offer me I don't know how many Leahs, Goldas, and Fridas. Among all the pretty faces I'm taken with Rifka, Helen's cousin. Jean Harlow she's not, but doesn't have a Mae West temperament either! It is in fact precisely her sweet and lady-like composure which attract me. . . . You test gold with fire and women with gold, they say. . . . Rifka is modest and studies accounting at her relative Broslavski's school. Good profession, I think to myself. Husband and wife are one flesh that becomes separated when they have different pockets. A woman who knows how to count would be perfect for a man who only knows how to lose.

I telegraph my sister Reisl telling her I'll be in Warsaw in a week, maybe more, since I want to visit Lendov and it's a considerable detour.

The road back to San Leopoldino was much slower and more ragged than the fast getaway she undertook that fateful morning when she crossed the road of lush hedges, between home and the Gentile universe. Out in the open, she got the hurtful perspective of her surroundings. She was able to see herself from a fourth dimension. She tried to establish a trialogue. . . . I, we, from them. . . . It was also more cautious . . . pain grants a feeble certainty. . . .

Lodsz, Lask, Czestocjhowa, Przyiucha, Wloszczowa appear before me like a parade of desolate places. And even though I arrive pretty late in the morning, it seemed like midnight. The dirt main road, the one I took when I ran away so many years ago, is completely deserted, as if everyone were asleep in the middle of the day. Where are the people who live here? What happened to Meilaj, the one who whistled at weddings? Where are Pinchas Gros and his goat? Who or what came through here? What earthquake erased all of them from the map? Maybe a voracious fire crushed all the humans of Lendov?

Someone approaches and holds out a supplicating hand:

"Something to eat, please!"

Could it be? Asher? The owner of the sawmill? "Asher, why are you covered in rags?"

"Who are you?"

"I'm Mordechai, the *moil's* son."

"Oy yoy yoy. Hurry Blima! The Messiah is here! David and Alta's son has returned!"

I ask myself if it could be indigestion giving me a bad dream and causing me to hallucinate. The healthy and robust wife of the richest and most successful one of us in the whole town. Could she in fact be this ancient woman barely holding on to a rotting cane, crying and blessing me at the same time?

Then the ghosts begin to emerge from their dwellings. . . . That one must be Fleisher: from shoulder to shoulder, he's carrying the same pole with the very same containers from which he extracted the milk he sold to us. Only now they're empty! He who once was the bulky and healthy owner of six milking cows, now is nothing but an absent glance. Yes, yes, of course, I'm just dreaming. . . . And could this living skeleton without strength to hug me be Fresser, the glutton? Please, gottenyu, can I wake up now?

"Here, my son, buy this elegant Shabbat coat for whatever coins you wish to give me," and when I look deep into the eyes . . . Gottenyu! Give a look down here at your world for a minute! It's none other than Rachman, that burly foreman of the Pole Andrei Vikoski's possessions!

The only one who is unchanged and who I recognize immediately is Josele Nar. Each village has its idiot and his smooth face remained fixed in time. God does watch out for his idiots!

And the children, where are all the children? Where are the young people? I walk, as if on glass, between the supplicating beggars, until I manage to make out the House of Study, my father's synagogue. Three little cadaverous boys read from a book with frayed covers. The pages are yellow and so are their hollow little cheeks. Their ragged clothing is patched, as are the walls and the scarce furnishings of the place.

These are the guardians of the Sacred House? This the house of learning where finally the drawings made by Marcus of Paris, that mysterious painter I remember, have been erased? Their boots and yarmulkes are full of patched holes, but could their heads be whole, with the wisdom of innocence?

Luckily, the only thing they haven't sold yet in my town are the

Books. There I see them, on the rusted book shelf, backdrop to those dear creatures of skin and bones, who still follow god. . . .

Who are we kidding? This time there was no pogrom, no cataclysm, no earthquake! My neighbors were turned into spots and rags, slowly but inexorably. They took away even the little food they managed to grow by sweat and tears. When these dignified poor people began to dance, the musicians stopped playing. I see with horror the change in those who used to collect donations for orphans, sick people, refugees and who used to pass around the box of money to send and support the old ones in the Holy Land so that they could pray away their last days by the wall in Jerusalem. Now these are the lice-infested beggars who beg without shame, in order not to die of hunger. These who once gave in secret, as our Law demands, so as not to embarrass those who receive the charity are now . . .

If you lose all your money, you lose half your wealth, but if you lose your self-worth you lose everything. These brothers of mine struggled to sanctify their labors and god laughed at them! Once, angels of life would walk around the world and make sure all was well. Where are they now? Only the angels of death remain very busy in my village. Can you understand why and how those who were healthy and brave fled as from the plague? They scrambled looking for a corner, somewhere, where there might be a little peace, if not mercy. Go, fight with god about this!

Is this poverty? No, no, no. When weren't we poor? All of us, in fact. No, this is something else. A calculated hatred orchestrated to destroy a human being's self-respect. You see, they don't take away their bread, only their means of earning it.

And who starved them of their own self-respect? Don't ever mistake the culprit. The Germans haven't even gotten here yet! That's still ahead. . . .

No, it's our own Polish brothers, those ancient Christians who go back to the days when my *cúzaro* grandfather chose these lugubrious lands to settle in. Faded birds of yesteryear, who now change their plumage and call themselves Republicans. Oy gottenyu! If disaster is really blind, how come it always has such a talent for spotting us?

Those who come from America can see quite easily that Germany is at the threshold, ready for a state visit. And Poland reminds me of the man who, after killing his parents, throws himself on the mercy of the court because he's a poor orphan. Oy Poland! He who closes his hands to compassion and his ears to the cry of the poor will someday call and not be heard!

Hail Lech Walesa! I'm not a proletarian, nor a cocktail party leftist. I am, however, daughter, granddaughter, and great-granddaughter of Poles. Your language is my language. I adore your music and know your customs and traditions! I am also deeply devoted to your artists. Please accept my long-distance message of solidarity at this black and lonely hour, when the Gdansk dockyard workers have been militarized. With the multiplicity of loyalties that characterize all people like me, I salute you with words that are well known in Venezuela where we know that being free is the greatest privilege, second only to life itself. We join the ten million Poles you represent and chant: "That's enough!"

Listen, had it not been for Hitler, I could have been your neighbor, maybe even your victim. Yes, you see up until 1938, and for centuries and centuries, it was a custom, almost a daily habit, for hordes of your Catholics to assault my shtetls, massacring us without pity. Anyway, that's all over now. Mostly because there are no Jews left in Poland and those who stayed, those very few, take great care not to remember their origin and credo.

Anyway, hail Walesa! Poland grieves with solidarity!

Father, if you could have read this, if you at least could have guessed what I tried to say, would you have condemned me? would you have approved? You the tireless, vivacious talker, how come so silent suddenly?

It's so hard to believe you are no longer my questioner . . . interviewer. . . . ❖

Reisl and her boyfriend, Saul Shuker, who greets me as if he were already my brother-in-law, meet me at the Warsaw train station.

At once I breathe a sigh of relief learning that they're both employed in a Polish pastry shop. It takes me a while to accept that this beautiful lady is the little girl I left behind on that Shabbat night when I left Lendov—only to return. . . . Reisl has two rooms on the outskirts of town. The building is shabby, what you'd call a tenement. She also calls in the matchmakers. "Reisl," I say, "let me catch my breath! I just got here! Why such a hurry? I'm not leaving yet. . . ." After a few hours I understand her hurry. When the guests leave, after the tea and cakes, we remain silent.

"Listen, little brother. Ruth Kramer, you know, the one with green eyes, well, her parents lost their store and all their money."

"Did they go bankrupt?" I ask

"Oh no! Nothing like that. No, the authorities just confiscated them."

"What authorities, Reisl?"

"Why the government, of course."

"They burnt down Sarita Cupershtein's family's food store, you know?"

"What's happening here?"

"Just what I'm trying to tell you. They beat up the Veingart brothers, right in front of their customers, because they dared to open the jewelry repair business after it had been ordered closed."

"I see. Just like in Lendov. Isolation. Privation. Death in life. . . ."

I decide not to scold Reisl any more over her matchmaking plans. To marry an American with his pockets full of money is an act of survival at this ominous moment. So, if I want, I can get the prettiest girl around. And even better, with a Venezuelan passport I have the right to leave immediately, if there is any danger. And believe me there is. Just living here is dangerous!

I honor my promise to you, Warsaw. I walk your wide avenues, I sit at your cafes dressed in a suit and bow tie, I buy poetry books and magazines, I go to the movies and to the theater. But, I'm a broken man, Warsaw! My clothing is offensive in the face of all the humiliation my people are living through. Truthfully, I can't enjoy myself at all.

So I, who shun politics, am persecuted by fate and forced to witness a frightening rally of the Polish National Democratic Party, right here in my very own cultured and distinguished Warsaw! The unstated objective of this march is to make clear how much we are abhorred. The crowd leaders raise their right hand to salute. Oh yes, they are well dressed and clean, richly covered in fur and wearing fine leather high boots.

The other Warsaw, ours, is locked up in panic in its cellars and dingy squalid rooms. Only a few brave ones leave the subsoil in order to wet their meager crumbs in the trickle of street water.

Mornings find me completely awake. I am unable to sleep for even a minute at night. Why did I come at such a time? Oy, my village! I should not have come back to your shadow, dear sweet Lendov. Markus? Markus in Warsaw? Is it you, the vigorous blacksmith, lifeless here in the Prayer House Hall? Zelig, you the happy shoemaker, now one of thousands of Warsaw beggars dragging around your skeleton under a threadbare shirt?

What can I say? I had to come back. No matter what, I had to come. How would I ever have believed it, if I hadn't seen it with my own eyes?

If you were still my analyst, dear examiner of mental trash, I would have to confess that my voluntary return to San Leopoldino, where the very intimate and the very hateful are part of the same complex knot, was extremely hard.

It's quite obvious that every day more and more of our needy immigrants arrive. All they've got is a wish to live. Next to these, many of their brethren are already middle class, and some even give themselves Finzi-Contini—like airs, as if aristocracy were a check made out to "bearer." . . . I guess it's O.K. for the original clápers to throw away what they earned by back-breaking labors, but some just show off the shiny shell; they pamper their descendants . . . us, really. . . . In some weird way, maybe deep in the display of mansions, jewels, and fancy cars lies a reaffirming wish to survive that is also mine. So, should I cover myself in lace, furs, and expensive gems in order to be part of the flavor, touch, smell, and shared feelings, which no matter what, I'll never lose?

There is a new and small sector of my community who arrive after the war and is even more pretentious. It boasts a nouveau richness. War trauma? They fight among themselves for the lead in the social pages of the newspapers, imitate all the vices of the so-called emerging classes, the ones drowning in all that easy oil.

Is it obligatory to become ridiculous, banal, and to go against everything one's inherited culture stands for in order to be accepted by this class of people?

Paradoxes, Doctor. What am I saying? Forgive me, Father, I got mixed up. I have returned rationally maniacal; now I am more like us and at the same time, more different and strange. Patched up and with the scars of deep surgery. . . . ❖

After a lot of begging, Reisl finally tells me where I can locate Erlich Mutnik, one of those comrades with whom we read about collectivism in the good old days of Lendov. His premature old age disarms me. We are seated in the office of one of the cooperatives that he supervises, and fueled by sour beer. After I tell him all about my experiences in America, I unload my heavy heart: "Can you please tell me who and how many members your illustrious Workers Party, the great Bund, actually has, since we have no artisans or workers left?"

"Stop thinking what you're thinking! There are fewer, that's true, but we're still here, aren't we?"

"And where might these others be? In Russia? Lithuania? Siberia? I don't see any here no matter how hard I look!"

"The struggle is hard. We just had a convention, right here in Warsaw."

"Who, the Bundist party, the workers, or the leaders?"

"Are you going to let me speak or are you going to go on and on with your sarcasm?"

"O.K., speak."

"We decided to remain vigilant . . ."

"And what about their famous agitation of the proletariat and their rage against our passivity, what about that, my friend?"

"We're fighting to weaken the fascist stronghold now allied with the Polish Socialist. . . ."

"I don't believe it! Although, I guess it could be. . . . In which case, the cat and the mouse make a deal over a dead cow. Is that what it is?"

"You're pretty smug, protected by a passport. . . ."

"Please, Erale, don't be like the bird who sees the grain but not the trap. You're a bit too old for that, don't you think?"

"What are you talking about?"

"About the fact that we are the preferred bait, always have been, ever since the days of kings and all the way to the Parliament of this republic, which would rather sacrifice us to stop Hitler, as they see it, but it won't be that simple. . . ."

"Better a bad peace than a good war!"

"I can't believe I'm hearing this from you! And what about the self-defense groups you formed year after year? Gone with the wind?

Because to tell you the truth I went to Lendov and all I saw there were ruins."

"And what was it you lost? Your grandfather's grand inheritance?"

"You're asking me? The antizionist defender of our culture which should have flourished here? Yes, Erlich, exactly, my grandparents' inheritance, that's what I lost."

I was repelled by his cynicism. Do you believe me? A party like the Bundists, that at one point had millions of militants willing to defend the use of Yiddish, the autonomy of our traditions, and our right to freely and publicly practice our religion in Poland, had turned into this. . . .

"Forgive me, Erlich, but did you switch parties?"

"Never. I'm the same as always. But these are different times. Our priorities are to look for tactical allies in order to reinforce our workers struggle, because your god is every day higher and higher and does not concern himself with these trivialities."

"I almost agree with you on that, but if I don't pray every morning thankful for the return of my soul to my body after sleep, I feel as if I had not brushed my teeth. . . . What I mean is, that god is under no obligation to find me sustenance. What's his, is his, and what belongs to the people is mine. . . ."

"Listen, the strategy for now is to consolidate against the Nazi threat. . . ."

Mutnik went to get more beer and I used the ten minutes to look at some pictures on the walls of this very narrow room, barely lighted by the waning light of a single candle. When he got back he brought black cigarettes which he smoked, one after the other, with uncontrolled anxiety.

"Listen, Erale, you know how it always is. Three centuries ago Cossack hordes led by Chmelnicki annihilated half a million of us. Two centuries ago, the peasant serfs—remember from our reading?—had their bloody and fiery revolt using an exact formula: on every tree they hung a feudal lord, a dog, and one of ours. What did your revolutionary comrades do? You know who I mean, the counterpart to today's Polirevolutionaries? You know full well what they did. When they ran out of lords for hanging, they opened all the gates so that the serfs could culminate their slaughter of our little villages from which the Christians had been warned away. Nu, am I right or am I right, Erlich Mutnik? I know Polish history better than you and I'm cured of all spooks. . . . Ot, ot, ot. That's exactly your problem. Soon you'll witness the next chapter. You know, if the victim is sufficiently fat—and we're already more than three million—the cat and the mouse will share the first part of the feast, but later, one of the two gluttons will turn on the other, and guess who . . ."

I thought I had him convinced because tears welled in his eyes—at least I thought so—and the corners of his mouth sank as if his face were a wrinkled parchment. I moved in and really tried to motivate him. "Erale, my beloved brother, why don't you go, and take with you as many of our people to the safe refuge of Palestine, Norway, France, wherever?"

"It's not so simple. Are you forgetting that we are almost four million."

"Not for single moment can I forget that. But each man is a life. Begin by saving at least one, yours."

"We would need large amounts of money to buy emigration permits. Few have it. Have you noticed?"

"I have, I thought you hadn't. They turned us into a nation of beggars and crazies."

"I suppose you mean those fanatic orthodox guys."

"No, I mean all. No exceptions. Even you. Yesterday I saw on Twarda Street a bunch of the religious ones. Nothing but bones studying like in the old days, while their wives sell sweets to the tourists. One of them offered me little breads, carefully making sure not to be seen by the Polish guards as violating the commercial prohibition that *your* allies have imposed on our people. . . ."

"It is the government of this republic which together with us will end with Hitler. . . ."

"And the women, Erale, have you noticed the women, still girls, selling everything, their pots, pans, sheets, candelabra. . . ."

"You're oversensitive, you've come from America the Golden. . . ."

Like talking to the wall. Mutnik turns a deaf ear, never really answering me. His large body, as powerful as life itself, is tied up by the strings of worn-out doctrines. He knows worlds, but I know what makes them turn. As I say good-bye I offer him money, in case he decides to leave Poland, but he turns me down violently, deeply offended.

When I finally make it back to Reisl's house, very late at night, I promise myself never again to argue about this with him or anyone else. Each must sleep in the bed he makes for himself. . . . My sister reminds me the next day that the following Sunday is the unveiling of our parents'—may they have found peace—tombstones. On that very sad hour when I see their names sculpted on the cold stone and I read the inscription, "May their souls be forever bound to the countenance of everlasting life." I think that I should put books and more books on Pappinyu's grave, just in case at some point he might feel like reading from the Sacred Texts while he roams around. . . . And on Mommala's I should put something forbidden. Bread and salt for her new home. And an everlasting flower. . . .

When we get back I ask Reisl to tell me all about their last days. She does so very sadly: "I forced them to come with me to Warsaw. Had I left them in Lendov, Poppa would have had to carry furniture on his back in order to earn the three pennies for the scarce food they consumed."

"Sure, that's what they intended to do. Destroy their morale and after that their bodies."

"Here they just faded away little by little like a plant with no sun or water, taken out of its natural surroundings, and so they went, as you know, within five months of each other. . . . They prayed from the moment you left. . . ."

"Listen, Reisyla, the other day I saw through a cracked window a cellar where a father, a mother, and two little children slept on the same mattress. A rat-infested hole without air or sun. Why, my god? Why?"

"Yeah, you ask him, maybe he'll answer you. . . ."

"No chimney, no heat, no stove, no wine, no water, in the bitterest part of winter! How will they make it to spring, Reisl?"

"They'll stay on that mattress for weeks in order not to freeze."

"So why don't you get out of here after you get married?"

"Where to?"

"To the Holy Land, with the help of the Zionist Organization or to Venezuela with me?"

"You're just like our brother Hershele. He wanted to take me to London with him when he left last year. What's your problem, impatient little brothers? Soon all this will return to the insecure peace of always. . . ."

"Isrul Hersh is smart. . . . What is it you're waiting for? You want to wait until you have to sell your chairs at the Gesia Ulica market in order to buy a piece of cracker? You yourself say Poppa and Momma blessed the day I left. . . ."

"They were so proud of your last letter where you wrote that you were a journalist and they cried over your articles. . . ."

"Didn't you drag them out of Lendov so that they wouldn't die of hunger? What do you expect for yourself? How long before you lose your job? Don't change the subject and answer me!

"It's different with me. They were ancient. . . ."

"Ancient at fifty?"

"Yes, they were. Calm down. This is a passing storm. You see darkness where there are only shadows."

Return to one's roots? And where might that be? Where's the point of departure? Let's see, Poland? France? Cuba? North America? Israel? Are we that ubiquitous? What about my most intimate memory? Can I find a golden, pacific America somewhere on the map? Is there a return? If so, to what matrix?

Yes, the creation of this history of a life . . . that's why, Mordechai Máximo, your fragmentary biography, a painting in sketches, is my small place of arrival in the world. Many will say there is no dramatic tension in this plot, that it is full of loose ends, that it lacks climax, a crime, that it's missing a rape, a theft, a pornographic scene. . . . How could there possibly be any intrigue in the story of a peddler forging a life for himself?

There was a time when I thought you came from nothingness, from a stupid little village, to perfection, toward this civilized existence. Now, I've discovered that it is I who am going from real nothingness toward the real everything . . . looking for you. . . . ❖

"Dear brother-in-law, We finally got married in November. Such a shame you couldn't stay a few weeks more in Warsaw and be with us. But what am I saying? You're with us all the time. Reisl and I thought of you a lot, specially that night, because we finally realized that you were right. Nu, so what's happiness without a tear for us, right? Well, in the middle of the dancing, Yeshe Horen, a family friend, comes from very far with the worst of all possible gifts. He tells us: "Not ten days ago, you should know, there was a terrible night of broken glass in Germany."

"Broken glass? What are you saying, dear friend?"

"Yes, just what I said. Broken crystal, belonging to our people."

"What's this all about?"

"Well, a young man from here, a student in Paris by the name of Grynszpan, found out that his parents were among those at Zbaszyn being deported to Germany. He became so enraged he wanted to avenge himself against the Germans. So you know what he did? He couldn't think of anything better to do than to assassinate Ernst von Rath, a high Nazi official in the German Embassy in Paris!"

"Gottenyu! He must have been crazy to do such a thing!"

"Well, the Nazis used that as the excuse they were looking for. They gave orders to riot all over the country. They began in Berlin by breaking the windows, shelves, and lamps in all Jewish shops. All in all, thirty-six killed, hundreds wounded, thousands jailed. Also, they destroyed houses, prayer centers, and books. High bonfires were to be seen in the middle of the streets fueled by the thousands of books taken from private libraries and places of worship. The streets were covered with broken glass. . . ."

Saul Shuker's letter softened by talking about friends and relatives, but I could see that fear had indeed moved into their hearts.

I had read about that incident in the papers and what frightened me most of all was the book burning. You know why? One of our thinkers, born in that very Germany, wrote that when books are burnt it is a sure sign that people will go next. Can you believe he said it a century ago? His name was Heinrich Heine. Oh yes, poets speak to each and all times, just the opposite of politicians.

Now it was known that the actions that resulted in the infamous Kristall Nacht found the Poles stranded over the border because the great Republic of Poland, allied with Erlich Mutnik . . . anyway it was several weeks before they were permitted to return and that only because of worldwide public pressure. I'll tell you that young Grynszpan reminded me of Samuel Schwartzbarad because that admirable lawyer Henri Torres, god bless him, was his defender too. How lucky I was to have seen him so close up eleven years earlier!

Shuker was right. I didn't want to wait for the wedding and as soon as I put stones on Poppa and Momma's tombs I returned to Kalisz because I realized I had left my heart there with Miss Rifka Warszawski, Rifkala as I call her. My chosen one came from a very honorable family and they simply refused to let me marry her.

She had become an orphan at a very early age, and was raised by her brothers who are very observant orthodox Jews like Poppa, may he rest in peace. I seemed a very bad candidate to them. They considered me a globe-trotting atheist, an adventurer in foreign lands, a man whose loud-colored clothes defied god. And worst of all, a crazy man willing to return to a barbarian country where the Indians eat white people alive! Another brother, a Red journalist, would probably take my side, but nobody knows his whereabouts. . . . I feel he's on my side though. . . . I did have a very noble ally in her sister Guta, who calls her Regina. She did admit that at first she didn't trust a man who could wear yellowish pants, green tie, and blue shirt, who furthermore did not wear his yarmulke, nor his long black coat, that solemn caftan that distinguished us from the rest of the population. Someone who always has his head uncovered and is so careless in his dress must be very fickle in his daily life, she confides. But when she hears the brothers' harassment and Regina's unhappiness she understands that destiny, so she says, has paved roads which no one can ignore.

One morning in 1945, she was woken up by strange noises. She went tippytoe to their bedroom door, unsure whether Father and Mother were crying or laughing. Is it possible to be dramatically happy? That must have been it.

Dad was repeating the text of a letter as if he were an automaton: WE ARE ALIVE. WE ARE ALIVE. . . . Guta and Abraham, WE ARE ALIVE. . . . The letter arrived at Box 163 Carmelitas Street to Max's name. How could her aunt have retained that information during those infernal six years?

Feverish arrangements to bring them to Venezuela made her mother crazy. And, she had just given birth to her third daughter, sickly little creature attended to by Dr. Gómez Maralet. This dear man had to listen with saintly patience to all the difficulties of getting visas for people unwilling to declare themselves Christian. . . .

The second daughter's name was Miriam, in honor of the maternal grandmother, and Pearl was the name they gave the last one, in honor of the Lendov grandmother, very much alive in their hearts. . . . Meanwhile, her uncle and aunt waited in Paris, cared for by Hela and David Haftarchik. They promised to tell us the entire miracle of their survival, and they did. . . .

The most hair-raising part of the Thousand and One nights they endured was the emotional retelling of a mistaken certainty. The couple spent almost the entire war in the same concentration camp, separated by a wire fence, taking for certain the other's death. Pulled from their families at Auschwitz's gates, they knew nothing of the other until that day in June, when Guta sent the WE ARE ALIVE. . . . They met on the main street in Konin, husband Hirshbein's home town, while each was searching for news of spouse and family. . . .

She promised herself to withhold judgment until the end. After hearing it, from their very lips, she swore she would always know that nothing could ever justify that genocide nor make up for such indignity. "Matters of State." "Nobody knew." "We thought they were factory smoke stacks." "We only followed government orders." "Who could imagine such things going on?" Lies which, on a daily basis, continue to legalize lawlessness and massacres in the East as well as the West. Of that very large family, only they are left to bear witness. . . . Oh, they did received a little note from Yehuda Ari, all the way from Siberia. He begged for news of the family and a little bread. . . . ❖

I want to leave quickly and take Rifkala with me. My other sister, Ana Bela, a widow living in Radom, comes to see me and offers good advice: "So let them test you on the Laws and the Sacred Texts, who cares? A son of our father, may he rest in peace, can handle any questions on religious matters."

What Anita suggested was done. On the appointed day, a representative of the Kalisz community was sent in order to leave official memory of the great event. For you I'll shorten the story; after all, the torture was almost two hours long.

"We have six hundred and thirteen precepts to govern our daily conduct, of which two hundred and forty eight say 'you shall' and three hundred and sixty five 'you shall not.' Why these numbers? Why not one more or one less, young man?"

"The first are equal to the human body's organs and the others make up the number of arteries and the days of the solar year. If we follow the rules, we make it possible for the human body to rise above the level of other animals."

"Do you believe and follow those precepts?"

"The day of the Final Judgment, we will not be asked if we believe in god, if we prayed, if we observed the rituals. The only question will be: Did you act honorably toward your fellow man?"

"Aha. And, do you by any chance even know how to pray?"

"Yes, I do, I know all the prayers required by Law. But what about the peasant who can't read the prayers but wants to pray on the day of forgiveness, and has a deep desire to communicate with god. His only way of doing this is a very passionate ki ki ri ki. If he lets loose that yell in the temple, is he or is he not praying to god?"

"Are you asking us or are you answering yourself? Don't forget that you are the one being tested here, young man!"

"Listen, brothers-in-law, or should I say stepmothers? Rifka will be well taken care of. Remember that Adam would not have taken a wife if first they had not put him to sleep. That's far from being my case. I'm taking a wife with my eyes wide open. And that's enough. I'm tired."

Well, they gave in unwillingly but it was the only way to handle them.

Ezekiel, the older brother, and his wife Frume led Rifka to the wedding canopy. Our wedding turned out to be the most sorrowful thing I had to live through in a long time.

I, the one who always clowns around at weddings, who plays my bandolin and sings and dances on tables, am somber and gloomy at my own wedding. It's not that it was obvious but I was oppressed by a feeling of definitive separation. And forgetting the happy reason we were gathered, I wanted to try to convince them one last time to follow me and Isrul Hersh and "sell some things, if not everything and get out or you'll be the first logs in the great fire. . . ." What did they answer?

"You're always looking for trouble!"

"Making up stories, in bad taste too, even at your own wedding!"

Nu, so . . . nobody is a hero in their own house. A deaf man heard and a mute told him that a blind man saw that a cripple went for water. They paid about as much attention to me as to last winter's snow. They laughed in my face. I was the pained clown of this sad circus. My father was right. Ignorant is he who wishes not to know . . . and he is the poorest of the poor. . . .

I also insisted that the last prayer be sung. . . . It was a piece by the composer Mordechai Gebirtig, which I had just learned in Warsaw. . . . My namesake wrote it in remembrance of the village of Prztytyk destroyed two years before by Polish peasants sent by the right wing of the Nationalist party. And it goes like this:

Se quema, hermanitos, arde
Oy! nuestro pobre pueblito ¡horror! se quema.
Vientos bravos con furia
rompen, quiebran y esparsen
aún más fuertes, las salvajes llamas.

Todo alrededor ya arde
y ustedes miran absortos, ensimismados
con las manos cruzadas.
Y ustedes, parados, miran quietos
cómo arde nuestra aldea.
Puede llegar el momento
en que nuestro pueblito junto con nosotros
desaparezca entre fuego y cenizas
y queden como después de una batalla
sólo paredes ennegrecidas. . . .

It burns, my brothers, it burns
Our poor little town burns
Oy oy oy! And the angry winds
Furiously break through, crush, and scatter the savage flames.
Everything around us is ablaze
And you stare, absorbed in thought
Hands crossed.
And you, standing, stare quietly
As our village burns.
The day may come when
Like our village we will disappear
Between fire and ashes
At the end
Only blackened walls will remain. . . .

Everyone cried. But Ezequiel scolded them. "Sha Sha Sha. It's a sin to interrupt the merriment of a wedding."

"Yeah, it's true, you always want to be contrary. All year round drunk and then, sober at carnival time!"

"Let's all follow and drink a toast! L'chaim! Mazel tov! To better times!"

"L'chaim! Mazel tov! Let's rejoice, let's forget, even if just for a moment!"

Once again I leave Poland, but this time accompanied and traveling by train to Paris. I'm sure I'll never return. Full of joy I leave with my wife. There is a key to each door and to each woman. Rifka is soft-spoken and hates noises. I'm as solicitous as possible. To cover up the shrieking noises of the wheels which balance us all this long tiring journey and to mask the terrible dizziness she feels, I sing to her:

Para mí tu eres linda
Para mí tu tienes gracia
Para mí eres la más hermosa
del universo. . . .

To me you're beautiful
To me you're graceful
To me you're the loveliest in the universe. . . .

and another one

When you're with me it's sunny
When you're not, it's dark.

But sugar in the mouth does not sweeten the bitterness of the heart. With the visit to Lendov I buried my yesterdays and who knows how much of my future. . . . I don't mention that loss to my dear wife. Words are like medicine, they must be used sparingly and carefully, because an overdose can harm and each medicine has a particular worth. . . . She, I must not forget, left behind the center of her being, to go to a different world, where, according to her brothers, women are kidnapped off the main streets and raped, and plucked the same as geese are plucked to make pillows. . . . Ah, a soft pillow, what all decent brides must have as their dowry. But no such luxuries for my Rifka. No, she travels with three dresses and without any feathery pillows. Without linens or precious stones. And who cares? I promise to support, honor, and encourage her always.

On board the *Amsterdam* we set sail toward my second discovery of America. . . . Rifkala, seasick all the way, is a passenger who does not know her vessel.

I think a lot and almost don't notice the storm. . . . Ten years ago I would have been praying in my cabin, now I'm smoking on deck. . . .

I return to America without money because I left everything I had with the family, like a cash offer for them to buy their salvation certificates.

I'm the most silent traveler on that boat.

I can't bear your silence. You force me to talk to myself as if I were crazy. My sedentary life is so poor in experience compared to yours. I've been a timid, cerebral wonderer. I belong to this parasitic and boastful generation, extravagant and injudicious with words. You stopped talking. You no longer argue. All you do is laugh. Forgetfulness envelops you, with your songs and poems, and these scattered notes in your beloved Yiddish. As I retrieve your journey, I'm looking to untangle my own. Your novel-like adventure has been to live. . . . My anti-novel misfortune has been to learn how to get along. . . . The perpetual Golden Chain. . . .

But Father, your voice, where is your clear voice?

To arrive once again with an empty wallet troubles me but not enough to keep me up at night. The slopes of La Guaira are the Promised Land and its little hillside huts are sumptuous palaces, a refuge of freedom. I need money to live, I don't live for money. I've seen more than one man fall apart while pursuing treasures, so busy in the pursuit, that he was unable to smell the flowers or hear the singing birds along the way. Too late, he notices his lost years but cannot recover them. He becomes weak and gets old accumulating wealth. For a fancy funeral maybe? When he tries to live, he is no longer awake enough for life. So, let that be a lesson to you. Grab your day! Night comes soon enough!

In Caracas I can work. Here I'll have a family. And what inheritance will I leave them? Simple. The knowledge that the spirit of a person is like a violin, and life a melody. Not everyone finds the right key at the right time. I tried to tune my chords day after day, in order to get the sound that pleases me. They say that he who finds it is very fortunate. One can spend one's whole life searching for it as I did, while others will insist you don't know how to live. Well, I know I'm alive!

Something saddens me, however. My songs are simple ones and will never be among the great truths left by poets. Perhaps one of my descendants will find in these simple verses a reason to go on, and that would be my triumphal crown.

I have to make a confession. Since returning to Caracas with Rifka I don't ask god for anything anymore. After all, he could suddenly get mad and say "Hey you! If you're so anxious for answers, come up here and get them!" and, what could I say? "Why should I want to go up so high? If I didn't die of hunger all those times, I certainly don't wish for the great honor of going up there now. Thanks for the invite, but I'd rather stay down here." Anyway, some things are certain: a tree can't be felled with one hit and two things become weak with age: teeth and memory.

But tell me something after all I've told you on this long, sleepless vigil, do you also believe I've lost the ability to remember? Of course my doctor persists with his pills for the circulation of the brain and memory shots. Which reminds me, he should be here any minute and I have to get my stupid face ready so that he can go on about some new syrup which decreases forgetfulness.

Listen, if you want to know something, don't ever ask the doctor, ask the patient. Time is the best remedy. It cured me of a disease that kills thousands every minute: the belief that happiness is money and more money. Between you and me, those who did not succumb in pain after receiving the news of the war dead drove themselves crazy searching for fame and glory. They succeeded.

They were honored indeed, and the weight of the praises, buried them all while they were still quite young. My Poppa David, blessed be his example!, used to say that the love of money leads to idolatry and causes insanity. How come my wise Grandmother Pearl, may she rest in peace!, did not name him Solomon instead of David?

You think I'm nuts, don't you? It's just that now, in my old age, I've got to hurry and quickly cancel everything outstanding because with every passing day there is less and less of me.

I distanced myself from those always looking for the cash-sounding and cash-feeling America. You know, just like new shoes: the cheaper they are the more noise they make. Anyway, you realize, don't you, that we come into the world with our hands closed but leave with them wide open, admitting that we take nothing?

Yes, that and much more. And probably too late. I wonder if anyone will pick up your compass and my belated zeal and use it to recharge and refuel their lives, making them as full of love for living as was yours. . . .

Your silent and slight shadow bears the weight of infinite yesterdays. . . . Is there a more lasting inheritance??

When a stone is left alone, it gets covered with mud. If you put it somewhere else, it could be stepped on and even shattered, but it suffers no pain. In fact, with time, the shattered pieces might have a use. One day a hiker finds the little stone, plays with it, begins to wonder where it came from. When he realizes that at some point it was smashed, he suffers for it. He holds on to the little piece of stone as if it were a living thing. And one morning he wakes up full of its energy, as I am now, on this first sunny morning in Caracas with my Rifka, or Señora Rebeca as they call her in Spanish. I realize full well how much I have to care for her, and yet money means about as much to me as the point of the sword destined to assassinate me. . . .

Obsessively I washed off the layers of dirt with which time had covered me. I was quite ordinary. One of those little stones you can find just about anywhere, picked up when, disillusioned, you walk with your head down. A hidden voice urged me to polish and keep polishing. After incalculable insomnia and fatigue, a brilliant diamond was discovered, but only by looking at it in the mirror could one see its full splendor. . . . Thank you for the legacy.

Of course if I, Mordechai, or Max, as they call me here, if I were to be born again, I would do the same silly things. No, that's not true. Nothing is ever the same. Just like I was never the same after I came back with Rifka.

I buy and sell, yes, that's still true. I'm willing to walk all over the hills of Catia, the valley of Aragua, the shores of the Guaira, to the Catuche of the Cabriales selling shoes that the Leiderman brothers give me on consignment. But I will never leave my sacred fire anywhere, like the Tiger that believes himself king because he caught his prey.

You've probably noticed that there are tall and short trees. Always dreamers, they make no trouble. They remain quietly by the side of the road, getting sun and rain. You can pluck their fruit, leaves and branches. They, on the other hand, don't take anything from anyone. They simply stand there. To fell them you need an ax and even then, who knows if you can reach the last, or the first, of its roots? The tree is born naked and then it gives flowers. When cold winds want to knock it down, it wonders if it will see another season. But there it is, still there, strong, supporting its own weight as well as the unmercifulness of others, without complaining. Patient and firm, it awaits the sun's return.

And here I am alone. Surrounded by so many ashes. Those who celebrated my wedding with me are now powder, calcinated in an enormous crematorium whose stench I can still smell and which at times chokes me. And I can't even inscribe their names or light a candle for their spirit. How is it possible for me to rejoice when I wake up each morning?

Hurry with speed, Mordechai Luzer of Lendov, son of David, get away from the mirror. You started talking to yourself, last night, Saturday, while watching the sunset and the first evening star, and now it's already Sunday morning when this home for memory-less old people opens its doors to visitors. . . .

Get away from the mirror, but clean it because it's filthy. Talking to yourself, you've remembered Lendov, Cuba, Paris, Warsaw, Caracas and for hours and hours, so many, in fact, that you've clouded it all with saliva, laughter, and tears.

Go on, keep walking, Mordje Luzer . . . drag your feet to the white hospital bed and take off your slippers before that nurse comes yelling: "And what are we doing up at this hour? Into bed, Señor Máximo!"

Go along, continue the pantomime. Remember each step. You don't know who you are, who you were, where you are, the name of this lockup, nor today's date because you've forgotten everything. . . .

In a few minutes your children and their mother will arrive with the grandchildren. And even though the circles under your eyes are deep and black because of the sleepless night, they'll all say: "How wonderful you look today!"

Remain silent. There is really nothing to talk about. Remember, keep smiling, after all you're a Freilich and you have to live up to your name.

You've almost realized your plan. From the little shtetl, a long and unrehearsed role. No public applause. To achieve that glory, you have to go on acting at every performance without pause or mistake. . . . You're a survivor of a world that disappeared and they all think that you're no longer among the living. . . . Well, ha! keep on believing that! I'm staying right here, waiting for the curtain to rise and to rejoice in all the bravos and encores. What is life after all, if not a great stage of perpetual revivals?

Finally, the last evening star is hidden and my night is ending. . . . I cleaned the mirror well and it's dry. . . . Come in everybody!! I'm . . . Freilich."